ANNABEL

"Finding Her Way Home"

~ A novel~

By

Alberto Mercado

To Belle
I hope you enjoy my book.
Alberto Mercado
11-16-10

ANNABEL

Finding Her Way Home

ISBN: 1453766286

EAN-13: 9781453766286.

Printed in the United State of America

The story in this book is a work of fiction and is a product of the author's imagination. Except for the character of Lucinda, any resemblance to persons, names, places or events is entirely coincidental and does not reflect anyone's life.

ACKNOWLEDGEMENTS

There are times in life when saying thank you is not enough. This is one of those times. I am so blessed to surround myself with people who are caring and understanding and always willing to lend a hand or just to listen without judging.

I need to thank my partner for his continued loyalty and patience with me.

To my editor who asked that her name remain anonymous, words can't describe how thankful I am for the work you did in this book. You took time away from your busy life to help edit my book, and for that I'll always be in debt to you.

A special thanks to my dear friend Lucinda. When it came time to write the acknowledgement page, as well as the tarot card reading on chapter seven, I couldn't think of anyone else but you to help me deliver something spectacular. Yours writing skills have always been an inspiration. All I need to do is give you an idea and you never fail to deliver the best. You are an amazing woman and I'm so honored to know someone like you.

To my friends and family for their continued support and for believing in me…Thank you.

The Trail, the Path, My Journey:

A road hardest to travel is the road we remember most. Anyone can walk or ride on smooth surfaces of pavement; this comes with no struggle at all. This paved road comes with no bruised knees, no thorns stuck to your thread-bare clothing or in your already sore and aching body. This road leaves no sharp pebbles stuck inside your half soled, torn shoes. One could hardly call this road a path at all. And this road certainly is not my story of my journey home.

My walk in life, like the ground under my feet, comes with many surfaces. While some of the roads have been covered with pine needles and soft, freshly fallen leaves, others, the ones less traveled, are the roads where points of view must be considered and decisions made. The longer the path, the more struggles I must face in finding my way to my place of peace and comfort.

My road was never one made of smooth-surfaced tar or hand-rubbed cobblestone, nor was my road ever a short one. I have walked this long, hard road and prayed for the day when I could actually look into everyone's eyes and say, "Thank you God for allowing me into your world. Thank you for walking with me, by my side when finding my path to home, and decisions are made. The longer the path, the more struggles I face in finding my way to my place of peace and comfort.

Do not go where the path may lead. Go instead where there is no path and leave a trail… Ralph Waldo Emerson

PROLOGUE

Right after my grandmother Helen died, I took my wife and daughter back home to Phoenix, Arizona. My uncle Felipe decided to move into my grandma's house. He wanted to make sure her garden was kept up to honor her memory. Her garden was one of her greatest legacies. She often used to tell me that life was like a garden: *"If you water just enough and trim the bad branches, you are bound to have beautiful flowers."* She was right. Tending her garden gave her much pleasure; it helped her endure the hardships of her life. Her home was filled with joy and laughter. Every time I came home to New England to visit my family I made it a point to stop by her house to visit with Uncle Felipe. We would sit on the porch and admire the garden. I would close my eyes and be transported, as if by magic, to the time when I was a little kid. I loved helping Grandma tend her garden. Her favorite plant was a rose bush that I bought for her birthday at a local store. I remember sitting outside on the stairs listening as she spoke to the plant. Amazingly enough, the rose bush remains the healthiest of all the plants in the garden.

"How I miss you, Grandma--- even after all these years."

These words started to sound like a broken record. Everyday since the day she died, I repeated those words to myself. From the time I was adopted, she made me feel like I had always been a member of the family; the entire family treated me as one of them. I can say without doubt that I am one of the luckiest people alive. My mother and father continued Grandma's legacy and raised me to be the best person I could be. My father Antonio, in particular, made sure that my childhood years were spent doing what children do best: having fun with toys, playing with other kids, and joining sports. He didn't want me to grow up too fast, the way he and his siblings did. Instead, he allowed time for me to be a child. It wasn't always fun and games. There were rules, chores and study time. None of these rules bothered me as much as having to go to bed at eight o'clock at night during school week. I hated having to miss my favorite television shows.

In spite of being adopted, I grew up without regrets, enjoying every minute of my childhood life. One thing I enjoyed the most was the fact that my parents, especially Dad, was always there for me. It was understandable given the fact that he never had a father figure in his own life.

While doing my college studies, I met Stephanie and soon after graduation we got married. Not long after Grandma Helen died, Stephanie and I found out we were expecting a child.

By the time I turned twenty-five, I was a successful architect working for a firm in Phoenix, Arizona. And although we both loved the financial freedom afforded us by our jobs and the agreeable weather in Arizona, we couldn't deny the fact that we were born and raised in New England. Every holiday season and every chance we had, we would pack our bags and fly home to Massachusetts to be close to our families.

Unfortunately, two weeks shy of our daughter Helen's fourth birthday, Stephanie got a call from her father. Rachel, her mother, had suffered a heart attack....

***

CHAPTER 1

Rachel woke up suddenly. She was sweating profusely and her heart was beating faster than normal. She sat up and looked at the clock-one-thirty. She could hear her heart beating. She looked at Carl who was sleeping next to her.

"Thank God I didn't wake him up," she thought.

She got out of bed and went into the bathroom. She took a face cloth, dampened it with cold water, and put it around her forehead and neck.

"These darn hot flashes," she thought.

After a few minutes, she started to feel better and walked into the kitchen to grab a glass of water. Half way there, she felt a pain in the left side of her chest and her arm became numb. Her entire body felt paralyzed, and when she tried to call Carl, the words wouldn't come out of her mouth. She put both hands to her chest. Suddenly the entire room became cloudy as her body plunged to the floor. The sound of her body hitting the floor woke Carl up. He looked over to his right and noticed that Rachel wasn't there. He looked at the clock, and then called her name, but she didn't respond. He jumped out of bed and looked in the bathroom, but she was not there either. Again, he called her, this time louder, but she didn't respond. He walked to the kitchen in the dark and almost tripped on something. When he turned on the hall light he saw her lying in the floor.

"Rachel, honey, what happened? Answer me Rachel."

He kept calling her, but there was no response from her. He ran to the phone and called 911. The paramedics arrived soon after, and she was rushed to the hospital. The paramedics told him that they thought she had a heart attack but couldn't be sure until the hospital did some tests. Scared and uncertain of what to do, he picked up the phone and dialed Antonio's home.

Antonio and Laura were sound asleep when the phone rang.

"Who could be calling this early in morning?" he asked. Laura who had been awakened by the call.

He got up and ran to the phone.

"Antonio it's me, Carl!" he heard Carl's frantic voice.

"Carl, what's going on?" Antonio asked.

"It's Rachel. I found her unconscious in the floor a few minutes ago. The ambulance already took her to the hospital. They think she suffered a heart attack. I'm so sorry, I just didn't know who else to call. I didn't want to scare the kids," Carl said crying.

***

That morning, my father called to give us the news. Rachel had been admitted to the intensive care unit. We made the trip back to New England again. Stephanie was heart broken to see her mother so ill.

"Honey, I'm not going to lie to you. The doctor didn't give us much hope. Your mother had a massive heart attack," Carl said to her.

Stephanie tried to compose her self. She wanted to stay strong for her father. She could see his pain, and it was breaking her heart. My parents, Antonio and Laura, were right by Rachel's bedside; our families have been close for as long as I can remember. When the doctor came to speak to the family, Carl introduced my parents as his brother and sister, and in the ways that count, they are.

My mother was inconsolable when she heard the news that Rachel might not make it. I sat alone for a while, thinking about the time we all sat in Grandma's living room awaiting her time.

"Fernando, are you all right?" my father asked.

"Yes Dad, I'm just a bit overwhelmed and saddened by all this. It's amazing how a person's life can change from one moment to another," I said to him.

"We need to be strong right now for Carl and Laura." Antonio said.

"I know that," I replied." I'm trying to gather all the strength I have to be supportive."

***

Rachel was well known in the community for her charitable work with the homeless and orphaned children, so it was not surprising to see people standing outside the church.

When the time came for me to give my eulogy, I took a big deep breath and gathered all the strength I had to keep from falling apart. I kept repeating my father's words for strength.

"We are gathered here today, not to mourn her loss, but to remember and celebrate the life of an amazing woman who was a wife, a mother, and above all, a true friend, not just to those who knew her, but to all in need…"

After I finished, I went and sat next to my wife Stephanie and proceeded to listen to my father and others speak about Rachel's life.

As with any funeral, it was hard to see those close to your heart suffering the loss of a loved one. After the ceremony, we all gathered at my parent's home for dinner. Carl seemed to be all right, although his silence had us all worried. He insisted he was just a little tired, and soon after he went home alone.

"Dad, promise you will watch over him. I know he is a tough guy, but I'm afraid he's going to hold it inside and that's not good," Stephanie asked my father.

"Don't worry. I'll make sure he's okay."

A few days later, Stephanie and I were back at home in Arizona.

***

CHAPTER 2

It was our daughter Helen's fourth birthday. Our house was filled with the laughter of children playing while the adults gathered at the kitchen talking about work and the heat of the summer. Later that evening, after everyone finally left, I put Helen to bed. The birthday party left her exhausted and she fell asleep quickly. I walked to the kitchen, grabbed a cup of coffee, and went outside to the patio. Where I found Stephanie standing by the pool looking at the horizon…

"Stephanie, are you all right?" I asked when she didn't respond the first time I called her name.

"I'm sorry honey, I didn't hear you," she responded.

"Today at the party a few people noticed that you were lost in thought. I think they understood why."

I approached her and placed my arms around her.

"I'm sorry Fernando. I haven't been sleeping too well lately. I…"

Her voice trailed off, and she couldn't finish the sentence. Her eyes filled with tears as she lowered her gaze to her hands. She gave me a hug, and we stood quietly for a while until she regained her composure and was able to speak again.

"I worry so much about Dad. Ever since Mom died, he hasn't been the same. Your parents told me that he doesn't leave the house at all, and they are afraid he could end up sick. I don't want to loose him as well, Fernando. He's all I have."

"What about me and your daughter? Don't we count?"

"Oh no Fernando, that's not what I meant. I'm talking about my side of the family. I know I can always count on you and your family. But my father is the only one left. I have no uncles, cousins or any relatives."

I stared at her hair as it was caressed by the evening breeze from the desert. If I ever had any doubts about the woman I picked for my wife and the mother of my child, those doubts disappeared forever. I took her hand and kissed it before pulling her toward me as we watched the sun disappear into the horizon.

***

It was Sunday morning and Stephanie woke up only to find that Fernando wasn't in bed. She looked at the clock- it was six.

"Strange, he hates getting up early on week ends," she thought.

The door to the bathroom was open and it was empty. Suddenly, she heard him talking with somebody in the living room.

"Who in the world comes to visit this early in the morning?" she thought to herself.

She got out of bed, went into the bathroom and brushed her teeth. She put on her robe and went to the living room. Fernando was sitting on the couch with the phone and his laptop. He looked up from the computer, waved hello with his free hand, and then signaled for a cup of coffee. "What in the world is he up to now?" she thought.

She brought him the cup of coffee and went back to the bedroom to make the bed. A half hour later he hung up the phone, closed his laptop and returned to the bedroom.

***

"Fernando, would you mind telling me what's going on? I'm lucky if I get you to wake up before eleven on a weekend, and here you are at six-thirty on the phone."

I walked toward her, kissed her forehead and asked her to follow me into the living room.

"Fernando, what is going on?" she said.

"Come sit here next to me," I said motioning with my hand for her to sit on the couch.

"Stephanie, when I married you, I made a promise to love you, to care for you and to make you the happiest woman in the world, right?"

"You are starting to scare me, Fernando." she replied with a frown.

I smiled.

"There's nothing to be worried about, honey. It's just that after yesterday's talk, I thought long and hard, and I came to the decision to move back to New England- only if you agree, of course"

"What!" she jumped up from the couch and stood in front of me.

"You can't do that Fernando, you have a great career, our home and besides, you love Arizona."

"Stephanie, Stephanie, it wasn't you who made me change my mind. All you did was help make my decision easier. I've been thinking about this for quite some time and yesterday's conversation just made me realize that there's no place like home. The money and weather might be nice, but we don't belong here; we belong back in New England with our family and friends."

"Fernando, you have me confused. What are you trying to tell me?"

"I'm saying that it's time to go home. I called my father this morning and told him of my plans. He told me that if we make the decision to come back, they'll be more than happy to let us stay at the pool house until we can find a home."

"What are you planning to do about your job?" she asked.

"My company owns a small sister firm back in Massachusetts, so I could ask them for a transfer there. I know someone just retired so I shouldn't have a problem getting the position. What do you think?"

"I don't know what to say. I think you just made me the happiest wife alive. Yes, let's do it. Let's go home!"

"My father is the only one who knows I have been thinking about doing this so let's keep it our secret and surprise everyone."

There was a sense of relief in our home once the decision was made to return to Massachusetts. This sense of relief helped us through all the preparations, packing and difficult good-byes.

A month later, we made the move back east. It didn't come without complications. My employer had already hired someone for the position I was looking to take back in Massachusetts. After a few negotiations, the company decided that I was too valuable to let go so they came up with a new position. My new position meant that I was going to implement and over-see new ideas and create more revenue for the company. Twice a month, I am required to travel back to Phoenix to report to my superiors, something I am willing to do.

After a few weeks of searching, we found a modest 1950's ranch style house for sale in a small town west of Boston. The house, while smaller than our former home, suits our needs. It is on a quiet tree lined street and has a large yard for our Helen to enjoy.

"Are you happy?" I asked Stephanie one night.

"I'm very happy. Just knowing that I can check on my father all the time makes me a bit more at ease. He act tough in front of me, but I know he's been crying."

"I know. I called him and asked him to come over for dinner, but he told me he had a headache, and he was going to try and go to bed early," I commented.

"Mom's death has been difficult for everyone, but he's taking it to very hard. They were so close to each other. Even last year when I came to visit, they were still holding hands and acting like high school sweethearts," Stephanie said with a sad smile.

CHAPTER 3

It was a cool afternoon and I was hard at work getting a presentation ready for plans to expand a local factory that would provide room for more equipment. This project is especially important to me, because if it goes through, our company would be in charge of the construction at a cost of five million dollars, which meant a successful business deal in my name.

"Fernando," one of his partners called.

"We are thinking of going to lunch at Pete's. Do you care to join us?"

"Thanks Mark, but I need to finish this project before the day is over. I'm going to be busy tomorrow with a new one and this is very important. Thank you for the offer, perhaps another time"

Mark nodded and walked away. I continued working at my computer, checking numbers and making sure that everything was in order. I didn't want to do give an estimate to the company and later find out that I miscalculated the financial aspect of the construction. That would result in a financial loss and a loss of reputation. A half hour into the project I started feeling hungry. I began to wish I had accepted the Mark's invitation, but it was a bit late to join them, so I decided to take a break and go to a new café that just opened down the street. It was a small place with about ten tables, nicely decorated, but not too fancy. I sat at a table by the window and picked up the menu. The server approached my table and greeted me with a smile.

***

"Good afternoon, my name is Annabel and I'll be your server today. Are you waiting for someone to join you?"

Fernando looked up and for some reason, his heart started to beat faster. He had a sudden feeling that somehow he's seen this woman before but he couldn't remember where.

"I'm sorry, you look familiar, have we met before?" he asked her.

"That's weird, I feel the same way. But then again, so many people have come to this café. Perhaps you've been here before?"

"No, I just moved to town from out west. I guess it's true what they say about everyone having a twin somewhere," he said with a smile.

"It's true. Can I get you anything to drink while you decide on the menu?

"Water would be fine, please."

"I'll be right back."

She walked away and Fernando sat there staring at her. He couldn't shake the strange feeling about this woman. He opened the menu and started looking at it. She brought him the glass of water and walked away to check on another table. After a few minutes, she returned with her note pad and pen.

"So tell me son, what brings you to New England? You look like a very important person with your suit and your computer, what is it that you do if you don't mind my asking?" she said with a smile.

"Thank you. I'm a district manager for an architecture firm out of Phoenix, Arizona. We opened a new office here not long ago, and I was appointed to the position," he replied.

"Oh so you're from out west then."

"Not really. I was born and raised here in the state, but I found a job and moved to Arizona with my wife several years ago."

"You look kind of young to be married." she said smiling.

"I'm twenty-nine and we have a four year old daughter," he replied.

"I'm sorry. I talk too much. I didn't mean to ask so many questions," she said apologizing.

"Oh no, don't be silly, I like to talk. Lately, all I do is sit at my desk alone and work on my computer. My wife tells me I spend too much time with the darn thing and that I should have married my laptop," he said laughing.

"Have you made your mind up what you want to eat, son?"

"Everything looks so good, I'm having trouble deciding."

"Could I recommend the soup of the day? It's very good. Butternut squash soup with ginger."

"Hmm, sounds like a good choice for a cool day like today. I'll have that plus a turkey sandwich," he replied.

She took the order and picked up the menu from his hand. She gave him a napkin with utensils and left his site. Fernando continued working on his laptop unaware that the server was staring at him from behind the counter.

She returned a few minutes later with his lunch. It was past one and the Café was almost empty.

Annabel gave him a faint smile and picked up the tray. "You better eat your lunch before the bread gets soggy. I'll be back in a few minutes to check on you"

Once again she walked away, and he was left with a sensation that this woman was hiding something, something perhaps too painful to talk about. After he finished his lunch, she came and picked up the dishes and gave him the bill.

"Thank you so much…?" he trailed off when he couldn't remember her name.

"Annabel is my name, and don't worry, most people don't ever bother to remember their server's name. Next time you come around, I'll test you."

"Ok, that's a deal. You have a great afternoon as well."

He picked up his laptop and looked around the table to make sure he didn't forget anything. Annabel went into the kitchen to see if they needed any help. She started cleaning the counters, but her mind was somewhere else. Seeing Fernando today brought her painful memories from the past.

***

I went back to my office and started doing some projects, but my mind was somewhere else. I stood by the window overlooking the town common. I couldn't shake the memory of Annabel and the mystery behind her eyes. No other person has impacted me as much as she had, and I was baffled by it.

CHAPTER 4

My father in- law Carl is a man who doesn't like to show his emotions in public. Stephanie said that in all these years she had never seen him cry until the day her mother died. After that, he became a different man. Suddenly, he found himself crying in front of us; at other times, he was more sociable and seemed to accept his loss. After Rachel's death, he kept to himself, only leaving his house to go to the market or for lunch at the corner café on weekdays, the same one I had discovered earlier.

***

"Good afternoon. Let me guess, coffee with cream, no sugar, then a club sandwich with mustard, no pickles? Did I get it right?" Annabel asked.

"You learn fast young lady. Perhaps you should be the one running this country," Carl replied.

"I'm not that young you know, but thank you, you boosted my self-esteem," she replied with a smile.

Three times a week, Carl bought the newspaper and drove down to the café right after the crowd had thinned out. He knew too many people in town, and he just wanted to be alone, to relax and read the paper. It was a routine even Annabel was starting to get used to.

"You know, you've been coming here three times a week for the past three months. I can read your mind when it comes to the menu, and yet I still don't know your name."

Carl smiled, took a sip of his coffee and looked into her eyes.

"Just the way Rachel used to make it."

"Who is Rachel? Annabel asked.

"My wife," he replied, not offering any further information.

"How come you never bring her with you? I would love to meet her."

"Well, she's indisposed right now. You see, Rachel is dead."

Annabel took a step back, surprised by his answer.

"I'm so sorry to hear that."

"It's all right. She was a wonderful woman; we had many happy years together. She always said that if you can't laugh, you shouldn't live either."

"I guess that's true, but you still haven't told me your name"

"I'm sorry, Annabel, my name is Carl Becker."

"How do you know my name?"

"Easy, it's written on your name tag."

Annabel looked at her tag and burst out laughing.

"I keep forgetting this darn thing is attached to me. Well, it's nice meeting you, Carl," she replied with a smile.

He nodded, but didn't say anything. He stared into her eyes, and although he didn't want to admit it, he found her attractive.

"Oh goodness! Let me go get your lunch. I think it's ready."

She left and came back right away with his lunch.

Twenty minutes later, she was back to pick up his plate and gave him the bill. He paid and waved his goodbye. After he was gone, she came back to the table to get the check and was surprised to see he had left her a twenty dollar tip.

She looked out through the glass door only to see him looking back at her; she smiled and waved goodbye.

CHAPTER 5

My father-in-law continued going to the same café on a weekly basis and his friendship with Annabel grew. Although my wife Stephanie continued to worry about him, I kept reminding her that her father was an adult and that he could take care of himself. Often on weekends, he came to our house for dinner and would sit in silence watching the game. Our daughter Helen was crazy about him. When Helen learned to talk, she started calling him Poppo and the nickname stuck.

"So tell me, Dad, what have you been up to lately?" Stephanie asked one night after dinner.

"Nothing much, I tend the garden, go shopping and stop at the café down the corner from Jonathan's three times a week for lunch."

"I go there often myself," I said. "The server is very charming."

"Hmm, how charming is she?" Stephanie asked shifting her eyes toward me.

"Oh Stephanie, she's old enough to be my mother. Besides, I only have time for the two women in my life."

"Well, that was the right answer; you just got yourself another get out of jail card," Carl replied winking at me.

"Her name is Annabel and she's very charming indeed." Carl commented.

"Dad, you even know her name?"

"Well, I did say I go there often, and she's the only waitress on weekdays for the breakfast and lunch service. It's not a very big place."

Stephanie and I looked at each other. I could swear we were both thinking the same thing.

"What?" Carl said defensively. "I only said I knew her name."

CHAPTER 6

"You're late today and you didn't come for lunch on Monday. I was starting to get worried," Annabel said approaching the table.

"I'm sorry, I forgot to call you and let you know." Carl said in a playful way.

Annabel went to the counter and poured some coffee before returning to his table.

"I had a dinner date with a special lady on Monday, and I'm late today because I went to bring flowers to the cemetery."

"You had a date? Who's the lucky woman?" Annabel asked.

"Oh, don't be jealous Annabel; it was my daughter. She took me out for Chinese food.

"Well, perhaps one evening we can go for dinner. I happen to love Thai food." she said with a smile.

"I'm not sure that's a good idea," he said, lowering his head.

"Come on Carl, I'm only asking you as friends. Besides, you need to stop living in the past. You're still young and handsome and there's a whole new life out there."

"I'm sorry, but I just can't."

Carl got up, put five dollars on the table and walked out.

"Carl, wait…." she called out, but he didn't look back.

Annabel stood there watching him drive away. She felt guilty, perhaps she spoke out of turn, but it was too late. * * *

A few weeks went by and Carl didn't come for lunch. Annabel kept looking at her watch staring out the window looking for his car.

"Are you expecting anyone?" the owner of the café asked.

"Well, kind of. I'm worried, John. Mr. Becker hasn't come by in few weeks, and he never fails to show up for his coffee and lunch."

"Why is it so important to you?" Customers come and go all the time. Perhaps he found a new place to go."

"No, I don't think that's it. I'm worried about him.

John looked at her but didn't say anything. He shrugged and went back into his office leaving her alone.

***

I stopped by the café to have a bite to eat before running to Worcester for an important meeting with an engineering firm. I found the server standing by the window at the café. She seemed to be lost in thought.

"I'm sorry, how long have you been waiting?" she asked when she noticed I had taken a table.

"I just got in, don't worry." I replied.

She took a menu and brought it to me along with a cup of coffee.

"I heard my father-in-law is a frequent flier here," I commented, trying to break the ice.

"Who is your father-in-law?" she asked.

"His name is Carl Becker. He told me he comes here for lunch at least three times a week."

"I'm so glad you came in. I'm kind of worried about him. He always came for lunch. I haven't seen him in a few weeks. Is he all right?"

"He's fine. I spoke to him yesterday."

She didn't reply. She took my menu and walked away. She was obviously concerned about him, but I couldn't comprehend as to why.

She returned to the table a short time after with my lunch which she served without speaking.

"Annabel, can I ask you what happened between you two?"

"What makes you think something happen?"

"I know my father-in-law very well. He's not one to change his routine that easily."

She looked around to make sure no other customers were waiting before taking a seat across from me.

"Last time he was here, we were talking, and he told me his wife had died. He looked sad so I figured I could invite him for dinner one night, as friends of course. He got nervous and left in a hurry. He told me that was not a good idea. I'm afraid he took it the wrong way, but believe me; I had good intentions when I invited him."

"Hmm, I see. He's a very quiet man and trusts me, he'll come around."

"I hope so because I feel terrible that he left so upset."

"Well, I have to run, but I promise I'll speak to him. You seem like a caring person, and he needs to snap out of his depression."

I paid the bill and left the café. I could almost say I was smiling thinking about Carl and Annabel. I think there was more than just a good friendship growing in their hearts.

CHAPTER 7

My parents came on a Saturday morning and picked up Helen to take her to the Science Center in the city. This was a good opportunity to spend time alone with my wife. After lunch at a local restaurant, I took Stephanie for a walk down the street to shop for on some candles and spices for our home. As we walking, she spotted a small shop with the curious name of Tara Zen nestled in the back of a narrow street.

Tara Zen is owned by Lucinda, a Tarot Card Reader, and is filled with spiritual items.

Lucinda is fairly well known in this part of town. We later discovered that she is quite an unusual character, someone many seem to look up to for guidance. I did have to admit that I was kind of intrigued. Stephanie looked at me before looking back at the shop.

"Having a reading is something I have always wanted to do, but I could never muster up the courage to tell you, because I knew how you would react to my feelings."

Joking, I told her that: I just wasn't interested in seeing a saggy, old woman, who has a huge wart on the tip of her nose, wearing a long black skirt and a pointed black witch's hat. I added the fact that I thought it was most likely her house smelled moldy because the drapes in her dark, dank house are probably as old as she."

"Fernando, stop teasing!" my wife said, "I want to do it, come on, let's go in."

"If nothing else, this might be the kind of day that years from now we might look back on and laugh about. Besides, the shop looks like a little doll house; it's adorable, and it doesn't look the least bit dark and dank. How could it be? Look at how charming the garden is. I should think that the inside must be at least as charming as the outside," Stephanie said, pointing to the carefully tended gardens with their colorful flowers, shrubs, lawn ornaments, figurines and many-sized glistening globes.

Over the door was a colorful sign that read - Welcome to Tara Zen. We knocked at the front door. As we waited for the door to open, we continued to gaze upon the beauty and color of the gardens. The door slowly opened and there stood this tiny little woman wearing coveralls with a button-down denim shirt with rolled up sleeves. All of her gardening tools were somehow attached to her clothing. She took off her dirty gloves, shook our hands, and greeted us. As I shook her hand, I introduced myself and my wife to her. Still thinking there must be a more witch-like creature in the house, I proceeded to ask her when we could meet this Tarot Reader I had heard so much about. The middle- aged woman looked at me and said, "My friend, you just did." "I am Lucinda."

Stephanie was eager to look around the inside of this little house. The room was painted in unique pastels. There were unusual glass globes everywhere and crystals we had never seen before. One room had a very old looking yellow map of Europe. It seemed as if everything in that room was exactly where it was supposed to be. Except for Lucinda's hair, not one thing was out of place in this entire little house.

"Please forgive my appearance. Gardening work is not for high fashion garb and high heels," she said.

The tension I was originally feeling was now beginning to fade. I couldn't believe the finds in Lucinda's eclectic collection and the interesting decor. We realized how busy this woman seemed to be with outdoor work, yet we wanted so much to have a reading. Lucinda looked at us and asked if we had ever done anything like this before. We looked at each other and laughed. "No Lucinda, we haven't done anything like this before in our lives," Stephanie replied.

"Well my dear friends, there is no time like the time that stands before us-the power of now, that is. So if you kids are ready let us begin our work."

Offering refreshments before a reading has always been one of Lucinda's trademarks. She believed that doing so eases her clients from their inner fear.

"Never are these refreshments welcome at my Reading table," she said, pointing out a table set up with refreshments. "It's just too darn distracting."

We chuckled at her comment when Lucinda's wasn't looking. Although her back turned away from us, Lucinda said, "I heard that!" And she too laughed along with us.

After we finished our refreshment, she led us to another table set apart from the rest of the shop.

"I have just one small request of you; be completely honest with me as honest as I'm planning to be with you. If you wish to hold back on me in any way, you will stop the flow of all that is to come, and therefore, you are not only wasting your precious money, but you are also wasting my valuable gardening time."

"Well then, if you're all set, let's begin."

Lucinda sat quietly for a moment before shuffling the cards. She then proceeded to spread them in a pattern along the table. Meanwhile, Stephanie and I kept looking at the cards and then at each other.

"This reading is one of complete honesty. The cards that are laid out before me show one individual who has hidden a life and kept a painful truth for many years," Lucinda said, starting her reading.

"Who are you referring to when you said "to one individual who held a secret for many years?" I asked.

"A true reading leaves much work to be done by the clients to hash out and sort through in their time frame. Readings come in forms of wording by spirit. It is not a language we share in our every day form of speech. It comes from somewhere above. Let me try to make this a tad easier for you," Lucinda answered before proceeding to explain.

"There is a person out there who knows all that was done in the past to ease the lives of many. Her secret was to secure the fate of another to insure the safety and security of a being that was so innocent in all the choices she struggled with for so many years."

I found myself confused with that sentence. "Who could this person be?" I thought, but decided to wait before asking more questions.

"The card below center is the Page of Swords. Fernando, this card represents you and your belief that something in your world feels incomplete. Through this card I feel there is someone very young who is struggling to find his or her path. It is up to you to fulfill the unanswered questions which hold the key."

Lucinda stared at both of us almost as if she knew what we were thinking. I was about to open my mouth to ask what that last sentence meant when Lucinda lifted her hand to stop me from talking.

"The sword is your tool to do whatever it takes to unfold the mystery regarding this young person's survival. Your strength in uncovering the truth is what sets another's spirit free of past pain. So yes, Fernando, in essence, it is up to you to find the truth of this untold story. Who are you and how did you come into this family? The spirit tells me that there was not a normal progression of mother and child in the natural birthing process. Here lies the key in all that is to come."

I jumped up from my chairs and walked to the window. My hands were sweating and my heart was pounding. "This woman is telling me about someone I completely forgot existed, my birth mother." I thought.

"Fernando, are you all right?" Stephanie asked.

"Yes, I'm sorry. Please go on, Lucinda," I responded.

"Use your sword wisely. You must choose your battles carefully, if not, the war just may be lost. When I say war, this is a figurative form of speech. It is almost as if you are going out on a hunt; if successful, you come home with your hands full; if not, starvation can and will strike all those around you. Others depend on your good choices to build a better life."

"A sword is what gets you through. Be vigilant in your search, but do this task in the kindness of all ways. Goodness shall forever win. Anger can get the better of you and that is when control of the situation becomes yet another struggle."

Lucinda stared at me for a few minutes without saying a word. She kept looking into my eyes to make sure there wasn't any confusion before continuing her reading.

"The crowning card is The Hanged Man. This card represents both you and Stephanie. Its placement is important for reasons you will understand in time. You will learn of things you never knew existed. Things you never dreamt possible. There will be uncertainty in movement. When I say this I need to explain...all you see and all you create will come back to you in forms of the unexpected. I do not wish to have you live in fear, for the chips will fall exactly where they must in order for both of you to find what is to be yours. We are universally sound, one simple thing created by God. We depend on each other for survival. Your strength is what will persevere. If you live this in fear, nothing will be gained from this experience."

I'm so confused. Nothing makes sense, yet I find myself drawn to your words." I said.

"Please let me continue for there is so much more. You need not understand right now what the cards are trying to tell you. As I said before, everything is going to fall into place, and that's when you will begin to understand what I just said, "Lucinda said.

"The Card in upper left position is our card of the Subconscious Rising, the Four of Staves or Wands.

What I feel, see and hear is illness looming. The four of staves shows four wheat stalks. Three stand tall and strong, one leans on its side showing failure to thrive. If we do not cure the ill stalk, the rest may fail as well. I also feel there is one soul who holds the key to this stalk's survival. Search for her. This person becomes a very important source of information for you both as time passes."

"We can only work with the tools we have been given. I implore you to sharpen them. Hone in on this source. "I must say to you both -"expect the unexpected," she continued. "I know both of you must have many questions swirling around right now,"

" The Hanged Man is a card that can either work for you if used correctly - by seeing, touching, feeling and becoming far more in tune to nature, the wonders of science and our all powerful healing Universe, or it can turn you up side down if you let go of the obvious. You must live in the brightest of warm, loving light-for here is where your hope lies." Lucinda closed her eyes for a minute before she continued the reading.

"The Card in lower left position of the Subconscious is the Six of Staves or Wands. For both of you, this is a card of peace, and love, and enjoyment of the fruits of your labor. Open your hearts to this card and your rewards shall be many. This card shows that both of you are people of great integrity. Your work is never done, and yet you both handle this labor not as work at all, but rather as gifts from above. In this card, your souls by doing this work are rewarded ten-fold. It is all about the follow through. It begins at the left and completes itself all the way to the right. Only then will you fully understand how wonderfully you work together as one."

"What does all that mean, Lucinda?" Stephanie asked.

"Toil the earth, grow your fruits, dig and search for the truth for it is that very truth that will set you free, that's all," Lucinda said before continuing her reading...

"This card is the Path to Future Meaning. Each of the three final cards represents one of the upcoming months. God, Goddess and Universe will give me a peek into the future for this ever so limited time. I always feel so very humble for this amazing ability to see into the future."

"This card is the Four of Cups. Cups are the symbol of giving. Both of you have this amazing ability to give until it hurts. Here is one time you must learn how to hold back, for your strength cannot be poured out in a way that diminishes your inner light. You must learn a new way of giving to each other and to those around you that are ill and in much need of finding peace. Many moons ago Fernando, someone gave to you the gift of life. It is up to you to fulfill this person's need, as she in turn will fulfill yours once again."

"Are you talking about my birth mother?" I asked.

Ignoring my question, Lucinda continued the reading: "This card shows four cups rising, yet the head of the lovely lady seated before them is tilted in weariness. I can see so very clearly the result of your findings throughout all of this will have a very positive outcome for all those involved. Just don't get yourself so tired that your thought process becomes muddled. Both of you will need to work on all cylinders until your truth is revealed. The question of your birth mother cannot be answered for it lies in the hands of the future. Your paths lie within each of you. Only with your thoughts and actions will this path be built."

"The next card is the Card Covering Center which represents strength and fortitude. Here is where you must be ready for any and all that is to come. The name Ann or Anna holds a strong key in your understanding of just how fragile our lives truly are. Embrace the child who is all good. Carry no fear. Move in the direction of the light for this will certainly get you through the darkest of places when tread upon. Understand that a card of such strength and power will always rise to any occasion. Keep your minds and hearts open for all that will come your way."

"Again, there is no explanation I can give you because this is the future we're walking in; you both carry the answers within the palm of your own hands. Tread on hearts lightly, smile whenever you feel confused or down. Your smiles will be someone else's medicine."

"The final card is the King of Staves or Wands." she said pointing to the last card. "In this deck, we hold four kings. One is the King of Swords, as he rules with an iron fist. Another holds a cup. He is the gentle King who is adored by those in his kingdom as peace within is all he knows. The third is a king of Coins who rules only by all he feels he is worth. Because he has much, he believes that he is all powerful. He is so wrong. The fourth, King of Staves, does not fear getting dirty. He is the one who works along side the others, who has no qualms of tilling the soil when preparing it for a rich harvest."

"This is you. This is what you both represent. Nothing ventured, nothing gained. You must rule this in a constant effort, not giving up until the key to your past has been found. You both know the meaning of hard work. This task will be the hardest challenge of all--- a test like no other. Yet in the end, your prayers shall indeed be answered as the efforts of many rely on all you do from this day forward."

"I know what you might be thinking: this may all sound a bit sixteenth century to you. Trust me when I tell you: This is how our good earth has always worked, and this is how it shall continue on for many centuries to come. You must both play the role of Kings, for this too is yet another form of inner strength. Ruling the land is no different than nurturing a family. You must remember to love, for in the end, love is all there is. If your tasks ahead are carried out with honor and dignity his rewards for each of you will multiply in ways you never thought possible."

"This is the end of my reading. I gave you vital information. It's up to you both to use it wisely. It's hard to believe someone like me, someone you never met before. I only ask you to take a moment and think of what I told you. You might not believe what I told you now, but trust me when I say, my readings never fail. Fernando, you were absolutely wonderful. I saw you slump into a very relaxed position. This is how I know my work is done. I pray you see it the very same way. If you would like to share another cup of coffee or tea with me, we can do this now."

Stephanie and I declined the offer as we had so much to sort through. We thanked the Reader as she gave us her final words.

"God bless you both as you embark on this new journey. I promise you that your future, although uncertain, will be one of joy at the end."

Lucinda paused for a moment, then taking my hand in her own, she made one last comment: "Your grandmother, Helen-she's a beautiful spirit-and she wants you to know that she's watching over all of you."

I stared at her trying to figure out how this stranger knew about my grandmother and how she would know her name .I didn't say a word. I nodded and took Stephanie, who had become very pale, by the hand, and walked out into the street. Neither of us spoke a word about what had just happened. Finally Stephanie wondered aloud if she had made a mistake by urging me to see Lucinda. It was, after all, supposed to be just for fun.

CHAPTER 8

"Hi, I'm Annabel. I called yesterday to speak with Father Sullivan," Annabel said to the lady at the desk in the rectory.

"Yes, I'm the person you spoke to. Have a seat for a few minutes while I go get him," she replied.

For Annabel, it was all too familiar. The memories of her childhood life combined with that tragic moment twenty-nine years ago was more than she could handle.

"Ma'am, are you all right?" she heard the voice of a man asking her.

She turned around and saw a tall, slim man dressed in a black suit.

"I'm sorry; I didn't mean to scare you, but you didn't answer me the first time," Father Sullivan said.

I'm sorry, Father; I was just daydreaming. Childhood memories, you know. It's been a long time since I've been here," she replied.

"Would you like to come to my office?" he asked pointing at a door next to the altar.

He signaled for her to sit in the chair across from his desk.

"I was just about to have some tea. Would you care to have some with me? "He offered.

"Please, thank you," she replied.

There was silence for a moment. She looked around the room. It was like a library filled with books everywhere. The desk was cluttered with paperwork.

"Here you go, Annabel," he said handing her a cup. "So tell me, why was it so important for you to come see me? I understand you were born in Worcester."

"Father, do you remember hearing anything about a little boy who was left at the church steps twenty-nine years ago?"

"How could I ever forget that day? I was the priest who found that baby. It was my first week on the job as a newly ordained priest. This is my second assignment to this parish," he explained.

"After finishing the early morning mass, I stayed for awhile in order to prepare for the next mass. As I had to place some literature at the front entry to the church, I decided to go out the front door instead of the usual side door to the rectory. I thought I could hear a baby cry, but this is a city, and there are a lot of people walking up and down the street. I didn't think anything of it at first, but as I turned to head over to the rectory, the crying became louder. That's when I realized that something was wrong. I saw a bundle at the far end of the steps. It was moving and I could hear a baby sobbing. I knelt down and looked inside the blanket. My heart skipped a beat when I saw the child. I took the letter that was attached and started reading it…."

Annabel interrupted him just as he was about to say what was written in the letter she started reciting the entire letter:

"Dear God,

Here I trust you with my most precious treasure. I ask you to please keep my baby safe, and I pray that he can find a family that will love him and protect him the way I would if I had the maturity and the means to support him on my own. It breaks my heart to leave him here on these steps, but I have no choice. I'm afraid his father is going to hurt him when he comes home drunk at night.

Dear God, I made a mistake, but I brought this beautiful creature into this world, but I will not tolerate an injustice. So here I trust you with my baby so he too can have a chance at life."

As she finished saying these words, tears were streaming down her face, and lifting her head, she looked straight into the preacher's eyes and with a weak, soft voice she told him: "Father, I'm the woman who brought the baby to your church. I'm so sorry; I didn't know what else to do.

Annabel proceeded to explain to Father Sullivan her story in detail. By the time she finished recounting the events, she was crying inconsolably.

"Father Sullivan, I need to know what happened to my child. Do you have any information--who adopted him, where he is now-anything that can help with finding him," she pleaded.

"I'm sorry Annabel. I really can't help you with that information. The only thing I can tell you is the name of the person I spoke to at children's services. Most likely your baby was put up for adoption, and the orphanage will not give out the name of the family that adopted him," he said shaking his head.

She knew there was no point to continue asking the priest. His heart was hurting knowing she was another victim of destiny. She recovered her composure and gathered her belongings. She stood up, thanked the priest for his kindness, and left the office.

On her way out, she stopped and looked at the corner where twenty-nine years earlier she had placed her child. She quickly walked down the stairs and didn't look back. All she could do at this point was to pray for forgiveness and hope that her son had a good life.

***

CHAPTER 9

As with every Monday morning; Stephanie planned to drop off little Helen at my parent's home. After we moved back to the state, she had decided to work part- time at her father's real estate company.

"Fernando, could you please reach for the thermometer under the cabinet?" Stephanie asked me from outside the bathroom where I was getting ready for work.

"What's going on?"

"It's nothing; I think Helen is just running a low grade temp. You know how she is sometimes," she replied.

As she expected, the fever was a little high, but she reached for a bottle of medicine and gave her a small spoonful.

"Do you think she needs to be seen? I mean, it's been a long time since she's been sick," I asked.

"She's all right. All children are bound to get sick one day or another, and we've been lucky so far. I gave her something for the fever so she should be better soon," she responded.

An hour later, Stephanie arrived at my parent's house, and right away my mother noticed that something was wrong with Helen.

***

"Stephanie, is Helen sick?" Laura asked.

"She was running a low grade temp this morning, but I gave her medication. There's nothing to worry about. She never gets sick, really. It is winter and children do get sick," she replied.

Laura didn't say anything else. Instead, she reached for the bag and took little Helen in her arms. Waiving goodbye to Stephanie, she closed the door behind them and went straight to the bedroom. She put Helen on the bed and proceeded to get her things out of the bag. When she turned around, Helen was sound asleep, which she thought was odd because she never fell asleep that fast. Usually, she would run to the family room to watch her favorite cartoons and play with her toys. Laura covered her with a blanket and shut the light off, but left the bedroom door opened a crack so she could hear Helen if she woke up.

"What's the matter? You look worried," Antonio asked, coming into the kitchen to join Laura for a second cup of coffee.

"I'm not sure, Antonio. Helen doesn't look good today. Stephanie said she was running a fever."

"Don't worry, all kids get sick. Let her sleep, its good medicine," he replied.

It was close to noon when the telephone rang. Laura was pleased to hear Annabel at the other end. It had been some time since the two of them had spent time with each other.

They had met one Saturday afternoon when Carl invited Antonio and Laura for lunch at his favorite coffee shop. Carl and Annabel had been seeing each for sometime, and he was anxious for Laura and Antonio to meet her. Laura felt as if she had known Annabel for a long time. She couldn't figure out why, but Annabel reminded her of someone, although she couldn't tell who. Laura felt comfortable enough that she gave Annabel her phone number to so the two could visit together at some point. Since then the two women had spent time together, and Carl and Annabel often joined them on Annabel's days off.

"Hi Laura, its Annabel. I have the afternoon off and I was wondering if you were available to go out for coffee."

"Well, I have my granddaughter here with me, and she is not feeling well. Perhaps you could stop by the house and join me for coffee and lunch here."

"Sounds good, but are you sure I won't be a bother?" Annabel asked.

"Not in the least, I would be delighted to have some company." Laura replied.

At noon time, Annabel arrived.

"Annabel, tell me about you," Laura said.

"Well, I was born and raised here in Worcester, but my parents moved to California right after I turned sixteen. I spent my teenage years moving from one place to another. My father was what you might call a nomad. He hated staying put in one place for too long. At one point we lived in a shelter north of Los Angeles after he had decided to quit his job in San Diego. We packed the car and drove all the way there only to find out the company that hired him was on the verge of bankruptcy and that the job was temporary.

After a few months they closed and Dad was out of work again. With no money or place to live, we settled in a shelter for almost a month," she commented.

"Sounds like you had a rough childhood," Laura said.

"It was rough, yes, but that was the life I was accustomed to living so it was natural to me. What I hated was making friends because I never knew when I was going to move away. Instead, I lived a solitary life. My parents were good to me. They bought me toys whenever there was money available," she said.

"Where are they now?" Laura asked.

"My parents died a long time ago. Before they passed away, I decided to move back to Massachusetts to live on my own, but close enough to keep an eye on them. My father took to drinking heavily and developed cirrhosis of the liver which in the end killed him. I took my mother to live with me, but two months later, she died of a heart attack. We all agree that she died of a broken heart. She was so attached to my father that she couldn't bear living without him.

I was dating someone before my parents died. He was good to me and so we moved in together. I thought my life was heading in the right direction. Then he started drinking and doing drugs. He was spending more and more time outside the house and soon after, the beating started."

"Oh gosh, Annabel, I'm so sorry," Laura said.

"Me too, Laura! You have no idea how much I regretted meeting him. After a few incidents, I couldn't take it any more so I walked out on him. That was the last time I saw him alive."

"What do you mean?" Laura asked.

"After I left him, I moved to California. I took classes at night while working full time at a grocery store. Finally, after receiving my certification as a medical assistant, I started working for a local hospital. One morning while reading the paper, I came across a report of a man who was involved in a car accident while driving under the influence who was in a coma. His picture was posted in the report. I called a friend of mine who was working at the hospital, and she told me that there was no chance for him to recover. A few days after that call, he died. In spite of everything he put me through; I still managed to mourn his death. I spent too many years with him, and it was sad to know his life had been wasted away with drugs and alcohol," she said looking down at the cup of tea she was nursing between her hands. Laura could see how much pain it was causing her to remember these past events.

"Annabel, I'm sorry, I didn't realize how painful it was for you to talk about your past," Laura said apologizing.

"Don't worry about it; in a way, it feels good to talk about it. It's like therapy for my soul. Sometimes it feels good to let it all out," she replied.

"Come, I want you to meet someone," Laura said while holding Annabel's hand. She brought her into the bedroom where Helen was sleeping peacefully.

"Oh Laura, she is beautiful.

Annabel looked at the child and her heart began to beat fast. It was as if she was looking at herself in the mirror. She remembered herself as a child with the pink cheeks and curly blond hair.

"Annabel, are you all right?"

"I'm fine; I was just thinking that this little girl looks so much like me as a child. I still have pictures somewhere."

Annabel continued talking to Laura, but she couldn't stop looking at Helen. There was something about this child that also reminded her of her own.

***

CHAPTER 10

"Well, hello handsome. Did you decide what you want?

Annabel asked me as I looked out the window above my table.

"I think I'll skip lunch today and have a coffee if you don't mind."

"Is everything all right, son? You look a little stressed."

"I'm sorry, I'm just tired. My daughter didn't sleep well last night."

"I'm sorry to hear that, but when you have children, they are bound to get sick."

"Do you have any kids, Annabel?"

"I'll be right back with your coffee."

Perhaps it was my imagination, but it seemed that as soon as I asked her the question, she became nervous and rushed away from my table.

A few minutes later she came back with my coffee.

"Fernando, have you had a chance to speak with Carl? He still hasn't been around."

I'm sorry, Annabel. I've been busy with work and forgot. I have an idea, why don't you call him yourself."

At first Annabel refused my idea, but after a few words with her, I managed to convince her to take the number. I was pretty sure she would call him, because the last few times I've been to the shop, the first thing she did was ask about him.

When I got home, I sat with Stephanie on the porch.

"I have a feeling, my dear wife, that your father is about to have a life changing experience."

"Why are you saying that?" she asked.

"Your father has a secret admirer and she is very interested in him."

"Who is she?"

"Well, remember the server from the Café? She's been asking about your father. Apparently, he told her he was a widower and she asked him out. According to her, it was just as friends, but he got upset and she hasn't seen him around in weeks."

"Well, listen to you, Mr. Gossiper."

"Not that I like gossip or anything, but I did managed to convince her to call him."

"Do you think she will? I mean, I'm up for it. Dad is lonely, and I know he likes her. I saw it in his eyes when he spoke about her."

"I know she will; she promised. I'm starting to like being a matchmaker."

I was happy to know that my wife wasn't against her father dating again. I think she was worried her father would end up going into a deep depression, and she didn't want to lose him.

We sat outside watching Helen play in the grass until the sun went down. I kept thinking how lucky I was to have such a wonderful family in my life.

CHAPTER 11

Every night since Rachel's death, Carl sat on his porch reminiscing about his past. He kept recalling Laura's words the morning of Rachel's funeral, *"Crying is the best medicine for your soul. Cry all you want because there comes a day when those tears will dry and the healing process will begin."* He did just that; he cried every night for a few weeks, and then the crying began to fade until one day, he didn't cry.

His thoughts kept shifting back and forth from his family to Annabel. He didn't know why this woman had impacted his life so much, and he felt guilty. His thoughts were interrupted when the phone rang. He went back inside to answer it. He looked at the caller ID, but he didn't recognize the number. "Hello, this is Carl speaking."

For a minute, there was a silence at the other side of the phone. He was about to hang up when he heard her voice.

"Carl, it's me, Annabel. I'm sorry to bother you, but I was worried about you because you haven't been around the Café."

"I'm sorry, Annabel; the truth is that I got scared."

"What are you scared of, Carl?"

"The unknown I guess. When you asked me out, I didn't know what to think. Honestly, I've been thinking about it. Perhaps I was wrong to feel so scared. I'm lonely Annabel, and I feel guilty saying that."

"Why don't you come by the Café around three? Maybe we could go for a walk. We all need friends you know."

After he hung up the phone, he felt a weight lifting from his shoulders. He's wanted to go see her, but he felt ashamed for walking out on her that day. NOW, he was feeling rejuvenated, and for the first time in months, he was anxious to leave his house.

By the time Annabel finished her shift, Carl was anxiously waiting in the parking lot... He kept looking at the rear view mirror to make sure his hair was still in place. When she finally came out his eyes lit up. She had changed into a pair of jean and a light pink blouse and her hair was down.

"Hello stranger. I hope I didn't make you wait too long.

"It's nice to see you again, Annabel. I thought we could go for a ride and eat in Worcester if that's all right with you."

"I'm game for anything."

He drove to the city and stopped at an Italian restaurant. During the ride, he kept looking at her, thinking how beautiful she looked with her hair down. The feeling of guilt had vanished from his mind. He had given Rachel many years of happiness, and although he still loved her, he knew it was time for him to give life a second chance. Not knowing what Annabel's intentions were, he needed to act carefully. They spoke during dinner and they laughed a great deal. The chemistry was there for sure. He felt good, he felt young, and he felt alive.

On the way home, they kept looking at each other without saying a word. He dropped her off at her house late in the evening. She surprised him by giving him a hug and a kiss in the cheek. When she closed the door behind him, Carl took a big deep breath and found himself smiling again.

The following morning, Annabel woke up to the sound of the door bell. She looked at her clock and noticed it was nine. She jumped out of bed, and after putting a robe over her shoulders, she went to the door. Not seeing anyone, she looked down and saw the package. Curious, she picked it up and looked around again before going back inside the house. She went to the dining room and placed it on the table and proceeded to open it. Inside was a small music box with a lighthouse on top. She held the music box close to her chest while reading the note attached, and she smiled; she hadn't felt so happy in years.

"Dear Annabel,

Thank you so much for a wonderful evening. You brought me back to life with your smile. I'm sure you're wondering why I gave you this gift. Well, I was hoping you would accept my invitation to go to the Cape this week end. I love watching the sunset, and I can't think of a better person to share that moment with than you. I know you don't have much time to think about it, but I hope you will say yes. I'll be waiting for your answer."

Carl

CHAPTER 12

"Fernando," Stephanie called in a panic.

"What's going on?" I asked.

"It's Helen. She is burning with fever," she said.

"Kids get sick all the time, don't be upset," I said trying to calm her down.

"I know, but she isn't responding when I call her. She's really lethargic," she said. "I'll go check her temp again."

She went in the room and checked Helen's temperature again: 103.

"Get her dressed while I call the pediatrician," I said.

"Fernando, its Sunday. The office is closed."

"Right, I forgot. We'll take her to the hospital then."

After getting ready, we took Helen to the emergency room at the hospital. The nurses took her right away, and after one of the nurses gave her a quick check-up, the physician came in the room. He examined the child and asked a few question before leaving the room. Fifteen minutes later, he came back to speak to us.

"I'm going to have to do some lab work to figure out what's going on. The fever should have gone down by now with the medication you gave her. The test will give us some clue," the doctor explained.

It was eleven o'clock in the morning by the time the results arrived. After a careful review, the doctor went back in the room.

"Well, the results of the blood work are back. I spoke with her pediatrician over the telephone, and he's on his way now," the doctor said.

"Doctor, what's going on with our daughter?" Stephanie asked becoming agitated.

"Please Stephanie, calm down. We still don't know for sure. Her lab work is abnormal, but it could be a result of many things. I prefer to wait until her doctor arrives so we can go over a few details first. I recommend not getting upset," the doctor responded.

"But doctor, it's my daughter we are talking about," Stephanie said.

"Stephanie please calm down, it doesn't do any good to get upset. The doctor is right. I'm worried too, but what can I do?" I said holding her hand.

"You're right. I'm sorry. It's just that she is so little; I hate seeing her like this," Stephanie said sobbing.

As soon as the doctor left the room, we sat next to the bed. I was aching inside to see my daughter hurting so much. I've seen her sick before but nothing compared to this. This was different and deep inside my heart I knew that something was terribly wrong. Helen's breathing was heavy; her face was red from the fever, and her hair damp from the sweating. I grabbed a dampened cold facecloth and placed it on her forehead.

"Fernando, call your family and let them know what's happening, but don't call my

Dad. I don't want him to worry right now," Stephanie said.

I left the room and walked toward the nurse's station. The nurse directed me to the waiting room where there was a telephone. I dialed my parent's home. When my mother answered it, I couldn't speak at first as I was overcome with emotion. I explained to her what was happening

"Did you speak to your parents?" Stephanie asked when I returned to the room.

"Yes," I responded. "I told them not to come until we find out what was happening."

A half hour later, Dr Cline and a team of physicians came into the room. By the look on his face, I knew that something was wrong.

"Please doctor, what's wrong with our daughter?' I asked.

"Based on the symptoms and the blood test results, I'm afraid that it's not good."

"What do you mean?" Stephanie asked.

"We believe your daughter is suffering from leukemia."

"I don't understand, Dr. Cline. She has always been so healthy."

Let me explain a bit about leukemia. Leukemia is cancer of the blood cells. It starts in the bone marrow, the soft tissue inside the bones. Blood cells are made in the bone marrow. A healthy individual's bone marrow makes red and _ white blood cells, and platelets. The white blood cells that help the body fight infections. The red cells carry oxygen to all parts of your body, and finally, the platelets which help your blood clot.

For one who has leukemia, the bone marrow starts to make a lot of abnormal white blood cells, called leukemia cells. They don't do the work of normal white blood cells, they grow faster than normal cells, and they don't stop growing when they should," he explained.

"So what you're telling us is that Helen has cancer?" Stephanie asked?

"I'm afraid . . . Yes," Dr. Cline replied. "You mentioned in her history that she had been feeling under the weather recently, not quite her normal self."

"Yes, but there's a cure for this, right?" I asked.

Dr Cline looked at both of us and then went over the papers hand.

"Hmm, well further testing will have to be done to see how progressed the disease is. For now, Helen will have to remain here in the hospital until we can get the fever under control. Also, her immune system is very delicate so she's going to need extra precautions. A simple infection could be dangerous in her condition." Dr Cline explained.

"Don't worry honey, we'll get through this. She's going to be all right," I told Stephanie, although I'm not sure she actually believed me.

Helen's fever finally broke so she was able to go home. We decided to wait for the other tests before informing our parents.

Carl and Annabel were getting closer. They were seeing each other more often. It was remarkable to see Carl's transformation. He was back at work in the mornings and had even joined a gym. Quite often now when we called him he would mention that had made plans with Annabel. We were all happy that he was getting out more often.

At the next family gathering, we informed the family of Helen's condition. The entire family was crushed, but it was Carl who took the news the worse. Stephanie did what she could to stay strong for him, but I didn't have the strength to face this disease that slowly was killing my little girl.

"Dad, don't worry, she is going to be all right. The doctors are doing everything they can," Stephanie told Carl, who was looking out the window in the living room.

When my father saw me struggling with this, he took me outside to the porch.

"Dad, I don't know what's going to happen. I'm trying to be strong, but I just don't know that I can handle it if something happens to her," I said crying.

"You have no choice, Fernando. You will get through this, you have to. Right now you have a child that needs you, but you can't help her or Stephanie unless you are strong. Gather your strength and help your wife deal with it. You know we are all here for you, but we can't help you if you're not willing to put in some effort. Leukemia isn't necessarily a death sentence today you know. Yes, it's a terrible disease, but there's been a lot of advancement in science, and many children get better with treatment," Antonio said.

"You're right Dad, I'm sorry. I should have learned something from your own life experience. I promise to be strong from now on."

"Come on, your mother is about to serve dinner and we don't want to spoil her cooking."

Dad put a hand on my shoulder and walked with me to the dining room where the rest of the family was already gathered.

"Oh Dad, I completely forgot about Annabel." Stephanie said, suddenly realizing she forgot to call her.

"Don't worry, I knew how preoccupied you were so I called her earlier and invited her," Carl replied.

"You really like her, don't you?" Laura said.

"She's been a great help for us. She never says no when we need her to take care of Helen, and she has a way with her that is magical. It's almost as if they share a bond. If I didn't know better, I would swear that they are related," Stephanie replied.

"Annabel is a great woman," Carl said quietly.

"You certainly won't hear anything different from us. She's really worked her magic with you, Carl. I'm not sure that you could have gone through all this without her. We have all noticed the change in you," Antonio replied.

Carl looked at him as if trying to figure out what he meant, but decided to brush the comment away.

"She is a good friend. She has always been there for me, and that's not to say that all of you haven't, because you have . . . I'm blessed to have such a wonderful family. But face it, you all have your own lives, and I'm not one for interfering. Annabel, on the other hand, she has nobody, and so we draw strength from each other," he said almost defensively.

"Now Carl, we all know that and we are happy for you."

Stephanie walked to her father and kissed his forehead. "I miss Mom, but I'm happy for you. I know this is what she would want you to do, to go on with your life."

"I just said that we are only friends," Carl said, looking a bit flushed. .

"Well, let's eat, dinner is ready," Laura announced. We noticed Carl's discomfort and were relieved to see that Annabel had arrived.

***

CHAPTER 13

"Dr Cline, here is the report you asked for on the little girl, Helen," the secretary said handing him a folder.

"Ah yes, thank you, Mary," he replied.

"If you're all set, I'm going to leave. All the patients are gone," she announced.

"Go ahead, Mary. Good night."

Dr. Cline sat at his desk and opened the folder containing all the reports on Helen. He studied them carefully, sometimes going back and reading them for the second time. After he finished, he put them down at his desk got up and went to the window.

"*Hmm, how can I tell them?*" he thought.

Dr Cline went back to his desk, and once again he opened the folder and looked over the paperwork. "What's this? I must have missed this part," he said aloud.

"Now, I need to figure out what to do." He closed the folder and called Helen's family, but nobody answered. When the answering machine picked up, he left a message for them to make an appointment to come see him. After he hung up, he closed his eyes and covered his face with his hand. "This case is so different than others. Where do I begin?" he said to himself.

The next morning Stephanie called the pediatrician's office and made an appointment for that afternoon. The secretary was already waiting for their call and told them that Dr. Cline wanted to see them at the end of the day when he was able to sit down and speak to them without interruptions. Fernando found it odd, but they agreed to come by at five.

Stephanie called Annabel in the morning to update her on Helen's condition. To her surprise, as soon as Annabel answered the call, her first words were to ask about Helen. Annabel always asked for Carl first so Stephanie was intrigued.

"I had a horrible nightmare last night. I dreamt that Helen was in danger and she kept calling for help.

Stephanie listened quietly as Annabel finished recounting her horrible dream.

"Annabel, I think you need to come over. I have something important to tell you," Stephanie said.

"Give me an hour to get ready. I'll be there soon," Annabel said, and then hung up the phone. She sat in silence wondering what was so important. Her heart started to beat faster than normal as she rushed to the shower to get ready.

After the phone call, Stephanie went into the living room. Suddenly, she felt her knees could no longer hold her up, and she had to sit down. Fernando came into the room and found her sitting down, pale as a ghost.

"Honey, what's wrong?" he asked.

"Dear Lord, I just remembered something that woman said."

"What woman are you talking about, Annabel?"

"Fernando, the tarot card reader, Lucinda! When she spoke of the four of staves, she said that three of the four stalks stood tall and strong, but one was on its side. It would mean that someone would be ill, and I didn't believe it, but she was right."

"Come on honey, you really don't think….." he said before she interrupted.

"Think about her words. I think she meant Helen. I have to try and remember the rest," she said.

Stephanie was exhausted. When she went to check on Helen, who was napping, she curled up beside her on the bed and fell asleep within minutes.

A half hour later, Annabel came to the house.

"Come, have a seat." Fernando said, pointing to a chair before proceeding to explain everything that had happened the previous few days. Annabel sat quietly, listening to him. She remembered that when she was a little girl her mother told her about one of her aunts who died at a young age from the same disease. At that time, there was little treatment for it.

"So that's what's happening. We still don't know what's going to happen. All we can do is wait and pray… a lot," he said.

"I'm sorry. I know how awful you both must be feeling. Is there anything I can do?" she asked holding his hand.

The touch of her hand over his own made him feel calm and relaxed, almost like a mother's touch. She had a way of making him feel comfortable and at ease. Whenever he looked into her eyes, he saw his own, and every time she smiled, he saw his daughter.

"Annabel, you have been very kind to our family, and we appreciate it very much. I have a feeling we are going to need your strength to get us through this ordeal. Stephanie is not taking it too well, as you can imagine," he said.

"Where is she?" Annabel asked.

"She went into the bedroom to check on Helen. Go on, I think it will do her good to see you," he said.

When Annabel walked into the bedroom, she found Stephanie sleeping next to Helen. She was holding her daughter's small hand and both were sleeping peacefully. She stood there in silence, watching them and wondering what it would feel like to have a child to love and hold. By now her child would have been the same age as Fernando. Stephanie turned and opened her eyes and saw Annabel standing there.

"Hi, I didn't hear you come in," Stephanie said.

"I just came in and didn't want to wake you up. You looked so tired."

"I gather you spoke to Fernando, right?" Stephanie asked.

"He brought me up to date on how she has been the last few days. I'm so sorry. I really don't know what to say, except that I'm here for whatever you need," Annabel replied.

Helen woke up and sat in bed. She looked full of energy again; the fever was gone. The doctors recommended everyone taking precautions when being near Helen because of her weakened immune system. Fighting infections would be tough for her and could take her life. Annabel went into the bathroom and washed her hands before holding Helen in her arms.

"Hello, little one. I heard you were sick, but don't worry, pretty soon, you're going to feel better. I promise."

"I already feel good, Annabel. Can we go play outside?" Helen asked.

Annabel looked at Stephanie for approval, but Stephanie shook her head.

"Perhaps we should play inside for now. It's still too early, and it's a bit cold," Annabel replied.

CHAPTER 14

"So where are we going today?" Annabel asked Carl.

It was a lovely day in early September, just a slight chill in the air.

"Don't ask any questions and just follow me. I told you it's a surprise," Carl said.

Carl took Annabel for a morning trip to one of his favorite places. She always looked forward to these trips because he seemed to know everything she liked.

"Here we are. Now make sure you bundle up well, the walk is long and steep," he said while putting on his hat.

"Where are we? She asked looking around.

"This is Moore State park. Most people come in the spring and summer, but I prefer the tranquility of fall and winter. Now come, I want to show you something." He said taking her hand and walking down the narrow paved road. Although it was a cool morning, the sun was shinning on the water making it look like sparkling diamonds. They arrived at what looked like an old mill. She kept looking around at the beauty of the place.

"Carl, this is magical, I feel as if I've been transporter back in time." she finally said.

"It sure is. I love coming here in the fall when there aren't too many people to spoil the serenity of the day. I've been coming here for years. It was Rachel's favorite place. Of course, she preferred coming in the spring when the flowers were blooming and the birds were singing welcoming songs on the warmer days," he said entranced in the moment, remembering the past.

"I appreciate you bringing me along. It must be hard for you to come here. You have so many wonderful memories of the times you had with Rachel."

"Perhaps if I was alone I wouldn't have been able to come here. But having you here with me is different," Carl replied.

"I don't understand . . . why?" she asked.

"In some ways you're much like Rachel. You both know how to appreciate the simple things in life. You are a wonderful woman, with values and a good heart just like my wife.

Don't get me wrong, I'm not trying to compare you with her in any way. But you compliment who she was."

Annabel blushed at his comment, and she felt his words deep inside. They continued to walk down the narrow path until they finally arrived at the spot where most photographers and artists do their magic with cameras and canvas.

"Oh Carl," she said in delight. "This is amazing. I can see why artists choose this spot. How can I ever thank you for this?"

"I'm the one who should be thanking you for helping me get through these tough times," he replied. She wanted to tell him how she felt about him, but instead, she remained silent, letting the cool breeze of the morning caress her face. She felt young again; she felt alive; and she felt loved.

CHAPTER 15

Every Sunday evening, Annabel sat home on the porch and wrote in her diary. Tonight she was feeling especially good. Her trip with Carl to the park was magical. Somehow, in the middle of it all, she was starting to have feelings for this man. She was confused, yet she knew there was nothing to feel guilty about. He was a widower, and she knew from experience that he was a family man, a good provider and a kind man.

Tonight however, was a special night. It was the twenty-ninth anniversary of that dreadful day she left her baby behind; she wanted to tell Carl how she felt about that horrible day she took her baby, wrapped in a blanket, and placed him on the step of the church.

My dear child,

It's been twenty-nine years since I last saw you, and trust me when I say this to you: there's hasn't been a year, a month, a day or an hour that I don't think about you. I have spent all these years living with the agony of having given you away. I remember like it was yesterday holding you in my arms and caressing your long dark hair. You weighed only six pounds, but boy, it felt more like twenty when I delivered you.

At first when I didn't hear you cry, I panicked thinking there was something wrong, but soon after, I heard your sweet cry. The nurse placed you on my stomach and you fell asleep. At that moment I felt like the happiest woman in the world. We spent the night in the hospital. The next day I tried calling your father to pick us up. After an hour of trying, I decided to call a taxi to bring us home. I kept making excuses for him. I told the nurses that he was on a business trip out of the country. When we got home, your father was asleep on the couch. He had an empty bottle of vodka beside him; his arms were bruised from the drugs. I tried to walk quietly to the bedroom, but you started to cry. I remember his reaction when he woke up. Instead of reacting like other fathers would when they receive their first son, he started screaming and cursing.

"Annabel, that kid is your responsibility, not mine. Make sure he keeps quiet so I can sleep," he said.

The first week you came home, all we did was fight. I tried defending you, but instead I ended up with a black eye. Most nights he got up in the middle of the night, dressed up and left the house so he didn't have to hear you cry. I had no money for formula, so thank goodness I was able to breast-feed you. This went on for a few weeks. One night, he came home drunk asking for food. I tried to explain to him that unless he brought money I couldn't go shopping. He got upset. He blamed it on you. He said that you were the reason why I couldn't go to work.

I promise you, it was not your fault. I blame only myself for allowing this man into my life. I blame myself for being so weak and for not getting rid of him sooner. I was so lonely back then. He was the only person I could count on, or so I thought. Anyways, that night, I took the worse beating yet. He grabbed me by my hair and threw me against the wall. Then he reached for his belt and started walking toward the bedroom to make you stop crying. I found strength from within and armed with a glass vase, I hit him on the head with all the force I had, and he collapsed to the ground. I wrapped you in a blanket, took my purse, and ran out of the house in the cold of the evening. At that point, I didn't care what happened to me: I just wanted you to be safe. I ran so hard that my legs started to hurt so much that I fell to the ground. I didn't know where I was. I looked up praying:" Dear Lord, I don't care what happens to me, but please, please help my baby. He's innocent of everything that's going on. Please, help him find a good home so that he can have a chance at a better life." As if by a miracle, I found the strength to stand up and walk again. Right in front of me stood the Church my mother used to take me to as a child. I went into the store next to it and asked for a pen and paper. I wrote a letter to the priest asking him to care for you. That was the most difficult decision any mother could ever make: to give up her child. But then again, I hope that was best decision I made, because if I didn't give you away, perhaps today you wouldn't be alive.

Twenty-nine years have passed, and although you're a grown up man, you will always be my baby. Maybe one day, if I have the chance to find you again and you decide not to forgive me, I'll understand. But know that I've loved you from the first moment I laid my eyes on you, and I will continue to love you until the day I die.

With love,

Mom

***

CHAPTER 16

A few months have past and our family has tried to live a normal life, although there is always fear in the back of our minds. Stephanie and I take Helen to the doctor once a week to check her blood count. Although her white and red cells continue to be abnormal, the levels have remained the same. The fevers however, continue being a problem, sometimes a few hours and sometimes days.

Christmas season was just around the corner. We decided to go shopping one Saturday morning and leave Helen in the care of my parents who were looking forward to spending time with her. It was always a wonderful time for them to have their granddaughter at home. My mother had a full day prepared for Helen since they don't get to spend that much time together anymore. First she was going to take her to breakfast before going to the science museum. Later in the afternoon, they were going to make Helen's favorite chocolate chip cookies.

We were still shopping when we got the call from my mother. At first it was hard to understand what she was saying because she couldn't stop crying.

"The ambulance is here now, and they're putting an IV in. She is still not responding," Laura said crying.

"Mom, please calm down, she is going to be all right. We are on our way and will meet you at the hospital," I said, trying to comfort her.

After inserting an IV in her arm, the paramedics rushed her to the hospital. By the time we arrived, doctors and interns were already doing tests on Helen.

"I'm sorry sir, but you can't see her right now. The doctors are examining her," the nurse at the desk said.

"We are her parents. Please tell them my daughter suffers from leukemia. They need to call Dr. Becker; he's the one taking care of her," I told the nurse.

"Actually, Dr Becker is on his way. We are aware of her condition, and they are doing everything they can. Now please, go have a seat in the waiting room. I promise, as soon as we know more, we'll let you know," the nurse replied before leaving the desk.

We gathered around the waiting room for what it seemed like an eternity. Mom kept sobbing and blaming herself for what was happening.

Mom told us what had happened. After they had been walking around the museum for a short time, she noticed that Helen did not seem to show as much interest in the displays as she usually did. Mom said she had asked Helen a couple of times if she was feeling all right. When she did not respond, Mom noticed that Helen seemed to be just standing there looking at a blank wall.

Mom repeated the question, but again, Helen didn't answer. That was when Mom became concerned and reached for Helen's hand just as she collapsed on the floor. Mom became frantic and started calling her name, but Helen was too lethargic to respond. Someone from the museum personnel ran over to help and called 911.

"I should have stayed home with her. Maybe it was too much for her for one day," Laura said, the tears running down her cheeks.

"Mom, it's not your fault. Nothing you did contributed to her relapse. Stop blaming yourself," I said.

Dr. Becker arrived and after gathering some information from my mother, he went in the room. It was twenty minutes later when he came out of the room.

"Well, the good news is that she is awake and doing well. The bad news is that the disease is progressing fast and her blood work is very high," Dr Becker said.

"What now? I mean, what can be done?" Stephanie asked.

"Well, there's only one solution, but it's going to involve the family," Dr Becker said.

We are listening. We'll do what ever is necessary if it means getting her healthy again," Fernando replied.

"As of right now, we are looking at only one option and that is treating her with high doses of drugs, radiation, or both," Dr Becker said.

"Unfortunately, the high doses from this treatment destroy both types of cells, leukemia cells and normal blood cells in the bone marrow." he went on to explain. "A better option would be a blood marrow transplant. New blood cells develop from the transplanted stem cells. The new blood cells replace the ones that were destroyed by the treatment. Helen is going to require a high dose of healthy stem cells through a large vein. It's like getting a blood transfusion."

"Can it be done on a child like Helen?" I asked.

"Absolutely! In fact, it's very successful. Helen will still need to have some radiation treatments and chemotherapy in order to kill her own blood cells and prepare her to receive the new healthy bone marrow," Dr Becker replied.

"Then, let's do it," I said

"No so fast, Fernando. There's one detail we need to discuss. For us to go ahead with this procedure, we need to find suitable donor with healthy bone marrow. Because Helen's condition is deteriorating fast, we will be unable to use her bone marrow. We need to find a family member or other donor with healthy stem cells. A brother, sister, or parent may be the donor. Sometimes the stem cells come from a donor who isn't related. We'll use blood tests to learn how closely a donor's cells matches her cells.

"How do we find out if we are a match, Dr Becker?" Stephanie asked.

"I'll do the paperwork for everyone to go get tested as soon as possible," he replied.

"Can we go see her? Laura asked.

"It's not recommended right now. I will allow the parents for few minutes, but the less exposure she gets the better it is for her. Right now, her immune system is very low, and I worry that she could develop an infection. That wouldn't be good in her condition, so I'm going to ask everyone entering the room to wear a face mask and gloves," Dr Becker replied.

When Dr Becker finally left the room, I looked at everyone in the room.

'Well, I hope nobody is afraid of needles."

"Fernando, there's one small detail you forgot," Dad said frowning. Dad had joined us soon after we arrived at the hospital.

"What's that Dad?"

"I'm afraid your mother and I might not be a match."

"What do you mean Dad?"

"Your father is right son. I know is easy to forget but remember we aren't your biological parents. It's going to take a miracle for us to be a match."

"Hmm, that might limit our chances. I forgot that detail," I replied.

"Well, there are still three of us anyway. I'm sure one of us will be a match," Stephanie said trying to elevate the mood in the room.

Early the next morning as I dressed to go into the hospital to be tested a sense of peacefulness came over me. I wish I could explain what was happening, but even though I knew my daughter was in danger, I felt as if something or someone was watching over us. By the time we left the house, I was completely calm and relaxed. As for my wife, she was nervous and restless in spite of my efforts to try to comfort her.

We arrived at the hospital ahead of schedule and went to the lobby to wait for my parents to arrive. To my surprise, they were the ones who were waiting for us. Soon after, Carl showed up and we headed straight for the laboratory. After signing some release forms, the technician explained the procedure, and one by one, he drew our blood. Once we finished, we hurried upstairs to check on our daughter. When we arrived at her room, Dr Becker was examining her. I saw vials of blood in the counter and another bag of IV ready to be hung.

"Dr Becker, what's going on, how is our daughter?" I asked.

"I'm afraid her condition is worsening. I'm sorry, I wish I could give you better news, but if we can't find a donor soon, I'm afraid Helen isn't going to make it. Chemotherapy is going to be our last option, but I do not recommend treating her without first trying to find a donor; it could be fatal for her."

The next few days were extremely long as we waited for the results. Stephanie had gone to the hospital in the morning while I stayed behind to work from my home office and to wait for the telephone call from the lab. I went into the office and sat at my desk by the window that overlooked our garden. Stephanie and I had tried our best to build a garden just the way my Grandma did, but it proved to be a bit of a failure. The only plants that were somewhat successful were three rose bushes my uncle gave us from my grandmother's garden and the only thing left of them were a few leaves. Everything else, including the grass, didn't make it past spring.

As I wrote some notes in my laptop I felt the same feeling I had experienced earlier. Suddenly, my whole body was relaxed; I felt as if something or someone was lifting me from the chair just the way a mother would care her child. As weird as it felt, I was not frightened. Instead, I was at peace, happy.

Everything was quiet. I had decided to go get a glass of water when out of the corner of my eye I saw a figure standing outside by the garden. I rubbed my eyes thinking the sun was playing tricks on me, and sure enough, when I looked again the image was gone. I continued walking toward the kitchen and grabbed a glass of water before returning to the spot where I had seen the figure. The glass of water I was holding fell to the floor and shattered in pieces. I found I couldn't close my mouth, and I couldn't move my body. The rose bushes, that minutes before were just about dead, were now blooming with roses like I've never seen before.

"There are beautiful, aren't they?" I heard a voice from behind me. At first I was afraid to turn around, but I knew I recognized the voice. When I did, I found myself standing in front

of my grandmother. *"That can't be, you're dead,"* I thought to myself.

"Don't be afraid my sweet child, it's truly me." she said smiling.

I was shaking so hard that when I tried to speak, my words were garbled.

"Grandma," I finally managed to say.

"My sweet child, I've never stopped watching over you and Helen. I know what you and Stephanie are going through. This will soon pass and better things are coming your way. Just know that I will always watch over you and your family."

I miss you so much, Grandma. You have no idea. I think of all the good times we had together. The cookies you and I baked in your kitchen. It's so hard for me to go to the house without missing you."

"Fernando, sometimes in life, we get caught up with the daily tasks and work, and forget to tell the ones we love how much we care about them. Would you please give the others a message for me?"

"What is that, Grandma?"

"Tell everyone how much I love them and let them know that I am always near if they need me. I'm very proud of each one of you, and soon my child, you too, will rejoice."

"I wish you were still with us; my daughter is in danger, and I'm afraid to loose her the way I lost you."

"You haven't lost me Fernando; I'm still with you in spirit. I was with you when you graduated from high school, and you thought of me. I was with you the first day in college. I was standing right there with you for all the exams. When you graduated, I was standing right there with you when you receive your diploma and I remember how you closed your eyes and quietly dedicated it to me. So you see I never really left."

"But Helen…"

"Helen is going to be fine. Now go and water my roses. They are getting dry. Only water them at night after the sun has gone down and fertilize them with lime at the end of the summer."

"I will, I promise. I don't know if this is a dream, but if it is, I don't want to wake up," I said, looking at her as if afraid to look away and lose her from my sight.

"I have to go now Fernando, but before I go I need you to promise me something.

"What is that, Grandma Helen?"

"Promise me that not matter what happens from now on, you will always open your heart without judging, and instead, listen to her."

"I'm afraid I don't understand what you mean. Her! Who is she?"

"You will know soon. Just know I'm always with you all."

As she said goodbye, her image dissipated into the air. At that moment I wanted to run and call my family, but I stopped to think first. Everyone is going to think I went crazy. Nobody is going to believe me if I tell them. Instead, I decided to keep what I had just experienced to myself. Armed with the information she gave me, I called everyone and told them to relax, that in the end everything was going to turn out all right.

Two days later, the family gathered at the hospital for the test results. Dr. Becker was at a conference that morning with his colleague. Instead, Dr. Roy was there with the papers.

"Well, is anyone of us a match doctor?" I asked.

Dr. Roy looked at the papers before looking back at me.

"I'm sorry, none of you turned out to be a match. I wish I had better news. We searched at the bank database as well, but we couldn't find a match there either," Dr. Roy said, apologizing.

Stephanie didn't take the news as well as I did. I believed my grandmother's words that everything was going to be all right. I was going to stand by her words. My parents were less surprised by the news. They had been concerned all along that those might not be good.

For the first time I thought of my biological family. Perhaps, somewhere out there, I had parents still living who might be a match and possibly, some blood related siblings or other relatives who could be a match.

"Don't loose faith; someone will turn out to be a match. I know my little peanut will be fine, I just know," I said to Stephanie smiling.

"How can you remain so calm when our daughter is lying in bed dying?"

"Stephanie, for once you have to trust me and believe me when I tell you that she is going to be fine."

She looked at me, and although she didn't say anything, I knew she trusted my words.

***

CHAPTER 17

It was a rainy morning and Annabel took the time to do some house chores. When she finished cleaning, she went down to the basement to fold her laundry. She turned the radio on and started folding sheets. She thought she heard someone call her name from a distance. At first, she thought it was the radio, but then she heard it again. Perhaps that someone had come into the house.

"Hello? I'm down here folding laundry."

She waited few minutes, but nobody answered. She turned the radio off and continued folding the laundry. This time, the cry came loud and clear…"Grandma, please help me." And twice more she heard the cry, "Grandma, please help me."

She ran upstairs and looked around, but couldn't find anyone. "Certainly, there has to be a child lost around here, I know I'm not losing my mind; I heard it three times," she said to herself. She opened the front door and looked around the yard, but couldn't find anyone. She was still searching around when the telephone rang so she went back inside the house.

"Annabel, this is Laura. Helen is back in the hospital."

"What happened? I just saw her a few days ago and she seemed to be all right."

"My granddaughter is dying, Annabel. We couldn't find a match donor for her bone marrow transplant. The kids wanted me to call you and let you know."

Annabel, dressed as fast as she could and left for the hospital.

When she arrived, Stephanie and Laura were alone in the room with Helen.

"How is she doing?" Annabel asked.

"Well, her fever broke which is a good sign, but she continues to be lethargic. She's sleeping a lot," Stephanie explained.

Slowly, Annabel walked to the bed and sat in the nearest chair. She brushed a strand from Helen's face and gave her a kiss on the forehead. It was heartbreaking to watch someone so small suffering from such a devastating disease; she felt helpless. Stephanie explained to them the different options they had when a group of doctors came into the room and asked them to step outside so they could examine Helen. Annabel got up from the chair, and as she turned to leave, she heard Helen speak.

"Grandma, I'm glad you came."

Everyone, including the doctor looked at Helen surprised at what they had heard. She had been sleeping all day and barely had energy left to speak.

"Honey, of course I came," Laura replied.

There was no answer from Helen. She had gone back to sleep.

Stephanie looked at Annabel, convinced that is was Annabel and not Laura that Helen was calling.

In the waiting room, everyone sat quietly, waiting for the doctor's report. Annabel sat next to Carl, but her mind was back at home. She was convinced that the child's voice she heard in the basement was that of Helen.

"Why would she call me for help?" she said, not realizing that she had actually spoken the words out loud.

"Who called you for help?" Carl asked.

"This is going to sound strange to you, but this morning when I was down in the basement, I swore I heard Helen calling me for help, and it wasn't only once but three times. At first I thought it was the radio, or someone coming in the house, but there was nobody there."

Maybe it was your neighbor's cat, they do sounds like children," he replied, not giving it too much thought.

Suddenly as if driven by her sixth sense, an idea crossed her mind. She excused herself, left the room, and walked down to the elevator. As she walked in and the door closed, the other elevator door opened and Father Sullivan came out, missing each other by a second.

Annabel knew exactly what she needed to do although she didn't know why. She went down to the laboratory and registered. The lab technician took her in the room and a few minutes later she was done with the testing. Now all she needed to do was wait.

She was about to go back upstairs when she spotted Carl coming into the lobby.

"I was worried about you. You left the room in a hurry. Are you all right," he asked her.

"Oh I'm fine, I just needed some fresh air, that's all," she replied.

"The doctors are in the room right now. Do you want to stop for coffee?"

"Actually, that's a good idea. I completely forgot to have breakfast this morning."

They went to the cafeteria and sat by the window. This was the first time Carl had seen her with her long hair not pinned up. He thought she looked so beautiful with light make up and a spring dress. "What?" she asked.

Nothing, I was admiring you. I think this is the first time I've seen you with your hair down."

"You hate it, don't you?"

"On the contrary, you look beautiful."

She felt her face blushing like a teenager.

"Well thank you. I haven't heard a compliment coming from such a gentleman since I was in my twenties," she replied.

"Annabel, can I ask you a personal question?"

She thought about it for a minute before she responded. She knew he wanted to ask her about her love life and she wasn't sure she was ready to respond.

"Sure, but I'm not sure I can answer it."

"Why is it that a beautiful woman like you is not married?" he asked.

"What makes you think I haven't?"

"That's true, but if you did, why haven't you talked about it? We've known each other for a long time, and I want to believe that I'm worthy of your trust."

"I was married once. I was very young and naïve. I thought I knew the man who swept me off my feet, and against everyone's advice, I ran away with him," she stopped for a moment; her mind seemed to have gone back into the past.

"Whatever happened to him?"

"The first few years we spent together were magical- we were in love. We didn't care about anything. We just traveled and partied like teenagers."

"Annabel, I'm sorry. You don't need to tell me if you don't want to," he said feeling guilty for making her bring up a difficult past.

"It's all right. I think it's time for me to unlock the door and let's the demons out. I have held on to these secrets for way too long, and if our relationship is going to go further, I want to make sure you know what you're getting into."

"All right then, so what happened?" he asked.

"He started going out at night and drinking heavily. Seemed like every night, he came home intoxicated. I tried telling him to stop, but he would become angry and hit me, so after a few times I stopped. Every night I would go to bed before he came home. On my nineteenth birthday, I woke up sick to my stomach. He was asleep from partying the night before. I got out of bed, trying not to wake him up, and ran onto the bathroom."

"But it was your birthday; he didn't take you out to celebrate it?" Carl asked.

"Are you kidding me? By then, his friends were more important than me. Besides, he didn't want me to find out that all our money was going into buying drugs and alcohol."

"Why didn't you leave him? Didn't you have family?"

"You could say I was blind at first. I was so in love with him and I wanted to save our marriage. Then came fear. I felt I couldn't go to my parents who were both old and sick. My father died soon after and my mother succumbed to depression. and She followed him a few months later. So you see he was everything I had.

"I'm sorry. This must be very painful for you," Carl said.

"Not as painful as what I am about to reveal to you. As I mentioned before, I woke up sick. I spent all day that way and couldn't figure out why. The next day I made an appointment to see my doctor." Annabel stopped and Carl could see how painful this conversation was to her.

"Annabel, you don't owe me any explanation. Your past is just that, a past."

"No, no. I want to tell you; I need to tell you."

"Why?"

"I'm tired of holding on to this pain that's eating me inside. I want to tell you because you've been so good to me and because…." She trailed off and turned around so he couldn't see her cry.

"Why is it so important, Annabel? Please tell me."

When he took her by the shoulder and turned her around to face him, he saw that she was crying.

"I don't know how it happened, but I fell in love with you," she said as her sobbing continued. "It doesn't matter though. After I tell you, you'll never be able to see me in the same way."

"Don't make conclusions based on fear, Annabel. Let me be the judge of that," he said.

"Well that afternoon, after my doctor's visit, I came home and waited for my lab results. Around four the doctor called with the news. He said I was two months pregnant."

"You have a child?" Carl asked, but she ignored the question and kept talking.

"At first I thought it would be a good idea for Jack to become a father.

"Perhaps he'll change his attitude once he becomes a father." I thought.

But when I told him, he went insane. He told me to get rid of it because he was not ready to be a father. I told him that I would not do that, but he wouldn't listen to me. Anyway, after that, things weren't the same. There were no good times. He became even more abusive. At one point he even questioned the baby's paternity."

"I still don't know why you stayed with him," Carl interrupted.

"I was alone in the world, I was scared of him, yet I was still in love, and I was sure once he saw the baby, he would change.

"Annabel, what happened to your baby?"

"Nine months later, I was home when I started having contractions. Jack was on his way out the door for the evening, so he told me to pack my bags.

He drove me to the hospital and dropped me off. I asked him to stay, but he said he had already made plans with his friends, so he left. At three in the morning, the baby was born - a baby boy. It was the happiest day of my life. I tried calling Jack to give him the news, but he didn't answer the phone. I spent two days in the hospital before being released. Not once did Jack come to see me.

When the nurses asked me about the father, I had to lie out of embarrassment. I told them he was a business man who was out of the country. I had them bring me to the lobby and told them that a friend was coming to pick me up. When the nurse left, I called a taxi to bring me home."

"Annabel, don't say any more. I can see how painful is for you to speak. I'll understand."

"No, I want to tell you," she replied.

"Well, if you insist then go ahead, but don't feel that you have to."

"When I came home, Jack was passed out on the couch. I woke him up so he could see his son but that proved to be a mistake. He screamed at me and told me to keep the brat quiet. One night, he threatened to place a pillow over the baby's head because he wouldn't stop crying. That's when I realized he wasn't going to change. I became frightened and feared for the baby's safety."

"Where's your son, Annabel?"

"One morning, I waited for Jack to leave the house. The night before he had threatened to hit the baby with his belt, but I was able to stop him and took the beating instead. I packed a bag with the baby's things and filled one for me. I wrote a note and left it on the table. I had no money and nowhere to go, but I knew I couldn't stay there. I walked for miles without a destination in mind. I didn't know what to do; I was so helpless, so I sat at the corner of a building and started crying. I prayed to God for guidance. Suddenly, I felt a breeze, and when I lifted my head, there was a church in front of me. A young priest came out to shake hands with the people leaving the service. He went back in and all I could do was hope that he would come out this way again. There were so many doors. I got up and walked toward the steps. I placed the baby down on the corner of the step where I hoped the priest would see him. I had written a letter explaining my situation and left it with the baby. I ran across the street and hid in the corner to be sure he found the baby. I felt such relief when he did because I knew he would take care of the baby. I prayed for forgiveness and for a good family for my son. I hated myself for what I did but I had no choice."

"Carl, I swear to you that I had no choice. Please believe me. There hasn't been one day in my life that I don't think about him, but I know that I made the right decision at the time. It has been a living hell wondering each day what has happened to him. Every year I celebrate his birthday; I wish that I could have done things differently.

"Don't torture yourself Annabel. What you did was an act of kindness. Life treated you unfairly. I would never think any less of you."

"Carl, thank you so much, you have no idea how much this means to me."

Annabel, why was it so important for you to tell me all this now?"

"Because I have fallen in love with you, Carl," she replied her head down.

"Annabel, I had fallen in love with you quite sometime ago, but I was so afraid to tell you because I didn't think you felt the same way. You have shown me compassion, love and understanding. You helped me get through one of the toughest times in my life. Of course I'm in love with you."

"Oh Carl, I'm so sorry. I swear I didn't mean to fall in love. I'm sorry I didn't tell you anything about my past earlier. I was so afraid people would judge me."

"That's nonsense. From now on, there won't be any secrets. As soon as Helen is better, I want to tell everyone about us, all right?"

"Sounds like a good plan Carl. You sound confident about Helen's health."

CHAPTER 18

The following day Helen's status remained much the same as the day before. The lights in Helen's room were dimmed and she was sound asleep. Once Father Sullivan finished praying and giving his blessing, he stepped into the hall to speak to Stephanie and Laura.

"Father Sullivan, thank you for coming," Laura said.

"How is she doing?"

"The doctors were here earlier. She desperately needs a bone marrow transplant in order for her to get better, but so far, we haven't found a match," Stephanie replied.

"You've got to have faith, my child; I'm sure they'll find…"

At that moment, the doctor came down the hall. He was smiling.

"I have great news. We seem to have found a match," he said.

Stephanie and Laura burst into tears of happiness.

"Do they know who the donor is?" Stephanie asked.

"We won't really know any information for a while. All I know is that the donor came to the lab requesting to be tested for Helen, which makes me believe the person knows the family." "I will have more details in a while. They are doing some genetic testing."

"What does that have to do with Helen? Well, that's where the situation get's complicated. It seems that this person has almost identical genes as Helen-which is extremely rare-based on the fact that the individual is not related to her. This is almost unheard of. Yes, there are people outside the family that carry genes close to that of the recipient, but in this case, the person has identical ones," the doctor replied.

Laura and Stephanie looked at each other intrigued as to whom this person might be. Regardless of that, the fact that there was hope for Helen took priority; Laura rushed out of the room to call her son and everyone and give them the news.

"See what I told you, Stephanie? The Lord works in mysterious ways," Father Sullivan said.

"Mom, is everything all right?" Fernando asked on the phone.

"Fernando, a miracle happened. They found a donor for Helen."

"Mom, I'll be right over. I have one more paper to do."

Fernando hung up the phone and started crying. This time, the tears were of relief and happiness.

"Fernando, are you all right?"

"John, they found a donor for my daughter. I'm going to finish this proposal and then I'm going to leave. I'm sorry to leave you alone."

"Oh no, you leave that to me and get out of here. Just tell me what needs to be done and I'll do it. You need to be with your family," John replied.

"Are you sure? I hate leaving you my work. Lately, I haven't been much help."

"Don't worry about anything. I know you would do the same thing for me. Now, go on, your daughter is waiting."

"Thank you, I owe you one."

CHAPTER 19

"Look who I found downstairs." Annabel told Stephanie and Laura.

"I'm so glad you're here," Stephanie said, as Annabel and Carl approached her.

"What's wrong, honey?" Carl asked.

"Nothing is wrong Dad. On the contrary, the hospital found a match for Helen's bone marrow transplant. They are doing more testing because of something unusual with the donor. I was too excited to understand all that science stuff, but the fact that we have a match for her is a miracle."

Annabel looked surprised. She hadn't told anyone that she was tested, and now she wondered if she was the match.

"Stephanie, did they tell you if the donor was a male or a female?" Annabel asked.

"The doctor didn't really say. Why?"

"Oh, I was just wondering, that's all. I'm so excited for everyone. Hopefully we can put this chapter behind us and Helen can begin to live a normal life again," Annabel replied.

"You are very thoughtful, Annabel. I'm glad you're part of this family," Carl said.

The comment took Stephanie by surprise; she wondered what he was trying to say.

At that moment Fernando came in. He had a look of excitement in his face that he couldn't hide. He could feel his heart racing. This day was a very emotional day for him and for everyone.

"Didn't I tell you not to worry; Grandma Helen was right all along."

Everyone looked at him with surprise..

"It's a long story, I'll explain it to you later. Right now we have to celebrate and give thanks to God for this miracle," Fernando said, barely able to contain his happiness.

"Can you please excuse me one moment?" Annabel said.

"Do you want me to come with you?" Carl asked.

No, Carl, you stay here with your family. It's only going to take me a minute.

She didn't wait for him to respond. She went to the elevator and disappeared behind the doors.

She walked over to the laboratory and saw the same receptionist who took care of her previously.

"Excuse me; my name is Annabel Baker. I was here yesterday for bone marrow testing."

"Hi! Of course. We've been trying to call you at home but couldn't reach you."

"I'm sorry; I was here in the hospital very early. I should have let you know. Is something wrong?"

"Why don't you have a seat for a moment and I'll go get the doctor."

Annabel was puzzled. "Why were they trying to reach her and why was the technician going to get the doctor?" she thought.

Before she could ask, the receptionist left the room. Annabel sat down and picked up a magazine. Five minutes later, the same doctor taking care of Helen came in the room and introduced himself.

"Miss Baker, come into my office so we can talk." Dr Roy said.

Once they got to his office, the doctor pulled a folder from one of the cabinets.

"Miss Baker, the reason we contacted you is because you had a blood test yesterday to see if you were a match for a bone marrow donor. Is that correct?"

"Yes, I'm a good friend of the family, and as soon as I found out none of them was a match, I decided to be tested as well. Is there a problem, Dr Roy?

"Well, it's not really a problem as much as a dilemma. You see, your blood test not only showed that you're a match, but your genetic testing is almost identical to that of the girl."

"I'm afraid that I don't quite understand what you're saying, Dr Roy," she said.

"We are puzzled because we've never seen anyone carrying almost identical genes between people not related to one another. I would almost say that's impossible."

"Well, I don't know what to say. I'm not related to them. My family came from the Midwest, and as far as I know, I have no family members around..." she stopped for a moment when she thought about her son.

"Yes, Miss Becker?"

"No, nothing, I'm sorry. I was just remembering something, but it's irrelevant." She replied.

"Hmm, well, now that we know that you're the perfect match for the girl, there's only one question.

"What's that?"

Are you still willing to donate some of your bone marrow to save this child's life? I'm not going to lie to you Annabel, the procedure can be dangerous, and you will need to go through some testing before you can donate," he said.

"I came to be tested for a reason. I don't care what it takes. That child deserves a life, and if I'm the one who can help her, then let's do it." Annabel replied.

Well, I'll go ahead and start the process. We don't have much time, so if it can be done tomorrow, will you be willing to do it?"

"Yes I am. You tell me when and where and I'll be ready."

"Great. In that case, I'll be in touch with you later on today.

CHAPTER 20

"Not sure what's taking Annabel so long. She should be back by now," Carl said.

They all stared at him without saying a word. They knew something was up between Carl and Annabel and they were happy for them. This past year had been tough for Carl because Rachel had been everything to him.

Carl and Rachel had met during their high school years; then he went away to the Navy for four years while she stayed behind to finish college. Upon his return, the first thing he did was to look for her. Since there hadn't been much communication between them, he was not sure if he was still part of her life. As soon they were reunited again, they knew that life without each other would never be the same. That same year they got married and a few years later, Stephanie was born.

Unfortunately, Rachel had a difficult pregnancy and there were complications during the delivery requiring a partial hysterectomy. Although they were sad not to have another child, they were thankful for this precious little girl born from their love.

"I'm still intrigued as to who matched Helen's blood," Fernando said.

"I can answer that question for you," Annabel replied from the doorway.

"Hey, I was wondering what was taking you so long," Carl said to her.

"I'm sorry," she said in a soft voice.

"What are you talking about?" Carl asked.

"Earlier in the week I went to the lab and got tested for a possible match for Helen. I really wanted to tell all of you, but I was afraid. I mean, I'm not part of the family so the chances of me being a match were extremely remote. I didn't want you to get your hopes up."

"Annabel, that is so thoughtful of you, but if you didn't think you were going to be a match, why did you go ahead and do it? I don't understand." Laura said.

"Laura, I just wanted to help in any way I could, and I thought that if I was a match and I hadn't done anything to help, I would regret it the rest of my life. I would never know unless I was tested. There was also that child's voice I keep hearing."

"What child's voice? Laura asked.

"I don't know how to explain it. I keep hearing a child's voice calling for her grandmother. I heard it at home, but when I looked around I couldn't find anyone."

"That's strange. Annabel, do you remember when you came in the room and Helen, still in her sleep, said, "Grandma, *I'm glad you came,"* Laura said.

"Laura, what do you mean?" Antonio asked.

"Well, I could have sworn she said that to Annabel and not to me," Laura said staring at Annabel.

"Annabel, when you walked in the door you said that you knew who the donor is," Stephanie said.

"I'm the donor."

"What?" Stephanie asked, not quite certain that she had heard correctly.

"When I went to get the results, the doctor was already trying to reach me at home. They said something about a link between our genes which I do not understand. But the important thing right now is that I can help Helen."

"This is all too confusing. I mean, I'm glad we found a match, but now this whole story of the genes is really strange," Fernando said.

Carl had been quiet for sometime, even through the shock of hearing that it was Annabel who was the match.

"That can't be," Carl said in a quiet voice.

"Carl, are you all right?" Antonio asked, noticing how pale his friend looked.

"Yes, I'm fine. Would you please excuse me?"

Carl left the room and went down to the lobby. He couldn't believe what was happening. Thoughts kept playing over and over again in his head, and by the time he got to the cafeteria, all the pieces started to fall into place. "It can't be," he thought as he poured himself a cup of coffee. "How can destiny play such a trick in our lives? Now what am I suppose to do?"

"There you are. You had us worried," Laura said approaching the table.

"I'm sorry Laura, I needed to think."

"Oh? Can you tell me what's bothering you?

"I wish I could, Laura, but can I ask you few question?" he said. "This is going to sound strange, but trust me, I need to know."

"What's going on Carl?" Laura asked puzzled.

"You told me once that a priest found Fernando at the church's steps, right?"

"Yes, that's correct. Why?"

"What else do you know about Fernando?"

"Well. They told us that a priest, actually, Father Sullivan, who's the priest in our parish congregation found him."

"Was it at Saint Peter's? Carl asked.

"Yes, they told us that he was wrapped in a blanket with a note attached to him; Carl, what's going on! Why this sudden interest in Fernando's past?"

"Laura, I don't know how to tell you but…." he started to say, when suddenly Antonio came into the cafeteria.

"There you are. What are you doing here?" Antonio asked as he joined them at the table.

"We are just talking, that's all." Laura replied.

"Carl, what's happening? You looked like you saw a ghost or something upstairs," Antonio said.

"I don't know. I'm so confused."

"Carl, I know something is bothering you. What is going on?"

I'm sorry. I can't tell you just yet. I need to speak to someone first."

"Dad, Mom, hurry! Helen's taken a turn for the worse. They are going to take her to the operating room," Fernando said in a voice that shook with urgency.

Everyone rushed back to the floor, but by the time they got there, Helen was gone from the room. Stephanie was alone crying in the room holding Helen's blanket. Carl looked around the room, but Annabel was no where to be found.

"Stephanie, where is Annabel?" Carl asked.

"A doctor came in and took her away. I guess they will have to do the bone marrow transplant right away if they want to save Helen," Stephanie replied sobbing.

"Okay, wait here, I'll go check."

Carl went to the nurse station and after asking for direction, he rushed to the room where Annabel was being prepared for the surgical procedure.

"May I please speak to her? It's very important; I need to speak to her before she goes into surgery," he asked the surgeon.

"All right, but only for a few minutes, we need to rush this procedure."

After putting on a face mask, Carl walked into the room and saw that Annabel was on the stretcher, ready for surgery.

"Carl, what are you doing here?"

"Annabel, this is going to sound crazy to you, but you're about to save the life of your granddaughter."

"Carl, what's wrong with you? Have you gone insane?"

"Annabel, listen to me. I wouldn't joke about this, not right now when her life is at stake. I have plenty of reasons to believe that Fernando is your son."

"But that's impossible, Carl. He's Antonio and Laura's son"

"Yes, but he's not blood related. They adopted him when he was only days old. He was found on the steps of the same church by Father Sullivan."

Silent tears were streaming down Annabel's cheeks.

"Father Sullivan, I know him. I just went to see him, but he wouldn't give me any information with regard to the case because of legal matters. I didn't know Fernando was adopted," she repeated to herself. "I have a granddaughter, Helen, and I'm about to save her life."

"Yes Annabel, he is your long lost son. I'm positive about that. There are just too many details and coincidences. And you have to think you and Helen carry almost identical genes which the doctors say is almost unheard of."

"Who else knows about this, Carl?" she asked.

"Nobody, I didn't want to say anything until I spoke to you. I know how sensitive this case is so I preferred to speak to you first. I was going to tell you tonight, but as you can see, the situation got worse. I thought that you should know before you went into surgery.

"Carl, do me a favor; please keep this information between us, for now I mean. Oh God, Fernando, my son…" her words trailed off.

"I'm sorry; we need to take her right now. We can't wait," the nurse said.

"Carl, take care of Fernando, and if something would happen to me, please tell him how much I loved him and the reason I gave him away. Also, take these keys, and if something happens to me, go to my house. In the dresser next to my bed, there is a diary. I want you to bring it to Fernando so he can read it. Carl, promise me you'll do that for me, please. And give little Helen a hug and a kiss from her Grandmother," she said crying.

"I promise I'll do what you asked. But you are going to be all right, I promise."

Annabel was taken away. He stood there watching as she was wheeled away through a set of doors.

He walked slowly back to the floor. He didn't know what to do. On one hand, he wanted to tell everyone about his secret, but then again, he would be breaking a promise he made to Annabel. "Don't let anything bad happen to my girls, Lord. I don't want to go through another loss," he prayed quietly.

CHAPTER 21

In most cases, a donation is made using circulating stem cells (PBSC) collected by aphaeresis. First, the donor receives injections for a few days of a medication that causes stem cells to move out of the bone marrow and into the blood. For the stem cell collection, the donor is connected to a machine by a needle inserted in the vein (like for blood donation). Blood is taken from the vein, filtered by the machine to collect the stem cells, and then returned back to the donor through a needle in the other arm.

There is almost no need for a recovery time with this procedure.

Because of the severity of the case, which left no time for Annabel to receive the injections, the procedure would be more complicated and dangerous for her. The surgeon would be required to collect the sample by bone marrow harvest. This meant that Annabel would have to go to the operating room and while asleep under anesthesia, a needle would be inserted into either the hip or the breastbone to take out some bone marrow. After awakening, she might feel some pain where the needle was inserted.

During the procedure, Annabel's blood pressure and heart rate increased, which added to the surgical team's concern. After they finished, the doctor decided to send her up to the ICU unit so that the nurses could keep monitor her heart for the night.

As for Helen, the procedure started right away. Bone marrow transplant is a difficult procedure to go through. The team began by administering high doses of chemotherapy and radiation to eliminate whatever bone marrow she had left and to make room for the new marrow transplant. Once the process was completed, the new stem cells were implanted in her body intravenously, like a blood transfusion. The stem cells would then find their way to the bone and start to produce and grow more cells.

The team of doctors working on Helen were extremely cautious because with this procedure serious problems can occur during the time that the bone marrow is gone or very low. Infections are common, as is anemia, and low platelets in the blood can cause dangerous bleeding internally. Helen was given a blood transfusion to treat these problems while she was waiting for the new stem cells to start growing.

The procedure went according to plan and Helen was wheeled back to the ICU unit.

"Well, I'm happy to inform you that Helen's procedure went well; she is rest peacefully. Of course, it's going to take time to find out if the procedure was a success, although I have little doubt. She is a fighter and her body is adjusting well to the bone marrow," the doctor told the relieved family.

"Dr Sullivan, what about Annabel?" Carl asked.

"She had some complications; her heart rate and her blood pressure went up. We are going to keep her in the hospital overnight."

"Can I see her?"

"Yes, of course. She is on the third floor. As for Helen, she will be in isolation for a few days. These are going to be very critical days; one small infection could be fatal. I suggest you be patient and wait to see her. I'll let you know more later on," he said before leaving the room…

Carl went upstairs and knocked on the door before letting himself in. Annabel was laying in bed sound asleep from the anesthesia. He walked toward the bed and sat in the chair. He held her hand with both of his, tightly, not wanting to let her go. He stared at her, trying to find something that might resemble Fernando and Helen.

"Gosh, this is crazy. How did all this happen?" he said to himself.

"Hi. What are you doing here?" Shouldn't you be with your granddaughter?" she asked, waking up.

"You mean our granddaughter?" he replied with a smile.

"She is doing fine so far, although we won't be able to see her for awhile. We have to be patient. And how are you feeling after all you went through?" he said with the concern he felt in his voice.

"I am doing amazingly well," she said. "I have to do well...I have a son and granddaughter to get to know. This is all so confusing, Carl. How did you find out?"

"I just put all the information together and it all made sense."

"What am I going to do now? I've have waited all my life to find my son and now, I'm scared," she said.

"There's no need for you to be scared. It's going to be all right, you'll see."

"You don't understand, Carl. I gave him up. I was not strong enough to fight for him. I should have kept him, but instead I took the easy way out."

You're wrong, Annabel. You weren't weak, you were unselfish. You gave up your child out of love, so that his father wouldn't harm him. You gave Fernando, your son, a second chance at life and for that, my dear love, you should be proud of what you did."

Carl heard a noise behind him, and when he turned around, he saw Fernando standing at the door, his eyes filled with unshed tears. Carl was about to stand up, but Fernando turned abruptly and left. He had come up to the room to see how Annabel was doing and to thank her for saving Helen's life. He had overheard the latter part of the conversation. He felt confused and his only instinct was to run away. He didn't know what to say or what to think.

"Fernando" Annabel called out to him.

"No, Annabel, let him go. I don't think we should try to stop him," Carl said.

"But…"

"Let him go Annabel, it's too late. Let him calm down. We can explain everything to him later," Carl approached the bed and sat next to her. He brushed a strand of hair from her face and kissed her cheek.

"I'm sorry Annabel; it's my fault that he found out this way."

"Oh Carl, you didn't know he was there."

"Annabel, what if he goes and tells the others?"

"I didn't think of that. Everything happened so fast. I have a feeling I'm going to have a lot of explaining to do," she said biting her lips.

"Let's not worry about that until we cross that bridge, all right?" Carl replied.

"Right now you need to sleep so that you can get your strength back. I promise I will help you deal with Fernando and the family when you are ready," he said giving her a kiss on the cheek.

CHAPTER 22

Stephanie sat next to Fernando's parents in the cafeteria. After a long day of waiting and wondering about Helen's fate, everyone seemed more relaxed. Stephanie looked exhausted. She hadn't slept at all in two days, and with no appetite, all she had been able to do was drink coffee to stay awake through the night.

"Stephanie honey, you need to try and eat something. This is not good for you, and now that Helen is out of danger, she's going to need you," Laura said.

"I know Mom but it's hard, I've had no appetite lately," she replied.

"Well, I took the liberty of ordering you a milkshake. At least that will give you some energy," Antonio said.

"Thank you; I'm so lucky to have you both in my life. I wouldn't know what to do without you two. I miss my mother, but having you both makes it a lot easier to deal with her death and all that has happened with Helen."

"I wonder what's taking Fernando so long. Do you know where he is?" Antonio asked.

"I left him by the lobby. He said he was going to make a phone call to his office before running upstairs to check on Helen and Annabel," Laura replied.

Stephanie looked toward the lobby and spotted Fernando outside in the garden. She thought it was odd for him to be out there.

"Well, I just found him." Stephanie said pointing toward the garden. "Excuse me for a minute; I'm going to go check on him. He's probably overwhelmed with everything that's been happening." She got up and walked outside toward him.

***

I stood there, with tears streaming down my cheeks. I couldn't believe the conversation I had heard between Carl and Annabel earlier. Is she really my mother? How can that be? I saw Stephanie approaching, but it was too late for me to try to cover the pain.

"Hey, what are you doing all alone here? We are waiting for you in the cafeteria. Is everything all right with Helen and Annabel:

What is going on?" Stephanie asked placing her hand on my shoulder.

"They are doing all right, but I just found out some shocking news about me. I know who my real mother is now."

"Excuse me? What do you mean your real mother?"

"My biological mother, the woman who gave birth to me, and the same one who left me at the church years ago; I found her."

"Fernando, now I'm confused. What are you talking about?"

"Come with me," I said, "I'll explain everything to the family at one time."

I took her hand and walked slowly toward the family table. I kept my head down, almost as if I was feeling guilty for something I didn't do, but I felt overwhelmed. I didn't know where to start.

"Son, we were waiting for you. Did you go check on Helen and Annabel? How are they? Aren't you hungry?" Laura asked unaware of the situation.

"Folks, it's a good thing you are sitting down, because what I am about to tell you is going to shock you."

"What's going on Fernando?" Laura asked.

"I found my birth mother," I said after taking a deep breath.

"What do you mean you found her?" Antonio asked.

I could see how confused they all were, especially my Dad.

"Just like that, Dad. I don't think I was supposed hear the conversation, but I overheard them talking about me."

What conversation? Who was talking about you?" Laura asked.

I looked at Stephanie for a moment then lowered my eyes before replying: "It was between Carl and Annabel. I overheard them talking about me. It wasn't my intention to listen in on private conversation; I guess you could say that I was at the wrong place and at the wrong time."

"What does my father have to do with all this?" Stephanie asked.

I didn't know how to tell her that her father was in love with the woman who gave birth to me. I thought that it was best if Carl and Annabel told the family that part of the story. I chose to ignore the question for now.

"Who is your biological mother, son?" Laura asked.

"It's…."

"Fernando." Carl approached the group. "Fernando, please, let her explain everything to you. That's the least you could do for her and truthfully, she deserves that right."

I wanted to answer him, but I couldn't seem to find the right words.

***

Suddenly, over the intercom, they heard the frantic call…

"Code red, third floor, room 15"

"That's Annabel's room," Carl suddenly realized.

Everyone ran upstairs, but the nurse stopped them from going in the room.

"I'm sorry, you can't go in there. There's a code red in progress."

"Nurse, what happened? She was all right a few minutes ago." Carl asked.

"We don't know. Her telemetry went flat. The doctor thinks she might have suffered a cardiac arrest, but we won't know 'till later. Right now the team is doing everything they can to revive her," the nurse explained.

For almost an hour the family sat quietly in the room waiting for the doctors.

"I think there's something everyone needs to know," Carl said.

"What's going on, Carl?" Antonio asked.

"The person who saved Helen's life, Annabel, she's the same woman who saved Fernando's life thirty years ago.

"What are you talking about, Carl?" Laura asked

"What he's trying to say is that it seems that Annabel is my birth mother," Fernando replied, looking at Carl for confirmation.

"Fernando, what you heard earlier is the truth. I'm sorry you had to find out that way. Trust me; we didn't know either until we put all the facts together."

"Carl, what is going on?" Laura asked.

"Laura, I wish we could have found a better way to tell you about this. What Fernando said to you is the truth."

"We should have figured this out ourselves. It is the only thing that makes sense," Laura replied.

Fernando sat there in silence, shaking his head and taking it all in, not knowing what to say.

"Carl, how long have you known this?" Antonio asked.

"Earlier this morning, before everything happened, I was downstairs talking to Annabel. She told me everything about her life and when I put all the pieces together, it all made sense. She had no idea either, and when I told her, she was shocked," Carl explained.

"Why did she do it, Carl?" Antonio asked.

"I think Annabel should tell you; it is her story, but please don't judge her. Everything she did was because she loved Fernando and wanted the best for him."

"Annabel is my mother," Fernando repeated, shaking his head.

"She couldn't have known that Fernando was her son because she didn't realize he was adopted," Carl said before turning to Fernando again. "Fernando, she loved you so much that she preferred to give you up for adoption than to watch your father harm you. Ever since that day, she celebrated your birthday each year. There hasn't been one day that went by that she didn't think about you."

"I don't understand. Why didn't she mention anything to me? We spoke so many times about our past, but she never mentioned anything about a child." Laura said.

"Apparently, Laura, you never mentioned the adoption part to her either because as I said earlier, she wasn't aware of it. She assumed Fernando was your birth child. Perhaps, the reason she didn't mention it to us was because she felt ashamed about it. She saw our close family, and she was afraid of what you might think of her, that we might judge her," Carl explained.

"I can understand that. But she should have known by now that we are not like that," Laura replied.

"Well, we can never be certain what others might think of us, and even from what Carl has told us, it sounds as though Annabel had little reason to trust anyone with her secret.

"I think I might have done the same thing," Stephanie added.

"I guess you're right," Laura replied.

Soon after, the team of doctors came out of the room.

"Doctor, how is she?" Carl asked the doctor who approached the group.

"Are you the patient's family?"

Fernando's father in law looked at him not knowing how to answer the question.

"Annabel is my mother." Fernando said feeling guilty because his mother Laura was standing next to him. He looked at her almost as if asking for forgiveness for hurting her, but she smiled and reached out for his hand her smile and a slight nod of her head showed him that she approved of his statement.

"And I'm her fiancé," Carl replied, looking at everyone.

Silence fell around the room and everyone stared at him. Stephanie walked toward her father and gave him a smile and a hug.

"Miss Baker suffered a heart attack. We almost lost her, but we were able to stabilize her," he said. "Tell me, do you know if there was anything that made her upset?"

"Well, kind of. It's a long story," Carl replied

"For now, she is going to need complete rest and a stress-free environment. Her heart is fragile and with the bone marrow donation, her immunity is low. Right now, she is not out of danger, and she could suffer a set back.

"All right doctor, we'll make sure she rests."

The doctor left the room. For a while no one spoke, no one knew what to say.

"We were going to speak to all of you as soon as Helen was better," Carl said.

"Dad, you don't need to explain anything. Besides, I already knew how you felt about her," Stephanie replied.

"We all knew it, Carl. We aren't blind. We could see the way you look at her and they way she acts when she's around you," Laura added.

"I don't know what's going to happen now. The situation is so different."

"Fernando, I swear we didn't know anything until this morning," Carl said, apologizing.

"Carl, you have nothing to feel sorry about. Besides, I've already made up my mind. Annabel saved my daughter's life. The least I can do is listen to her. I'm not mad at her. I'm just confused because everything happened so fast."

"Fernando, you're a good son. Your father and I are very proud of you. Please don't judge her until you know the facts." Laura said.

"Don't worry Mom, I won't," he replied.

"Fernando, we need to go upstairs and check on Helen. By now, she should be settled in her room, and I think they'll let us see her now," said Stephanie.

Fernando nodded and they left the room, anxious to be with their little girl.

"Laura, what am I going to do now?" Carl said.

"You can only do what your heart dictates. Your situation shouldn't change anything. We'll sit down with Annabel as soon as she recovers, and we'll take it from there," Laura replied.

"Thank you. I think I'll go and check on her. You go on ahead, and I'll meet you upstairs in a while."

Antonio and Laura left Carl alone in the room. He looked out the window to give himself time to settle his mind. It was with a sense of relief that right now, Helen and Annabel's health was the most important thing and they were both doing better. Annabel stood by him when he needed her most. Now it was time for him to return the favor. He was not going to leave her alone.

Seeing that the nurse was at the station, he approached the desk and asked if he might see Annabel.

"Hold one minute and I'll ask the doctor."

She walked to the back where the physician was doing dictations. They both looked in his direction and the doctor nodded. She returned to the desk and handed him a mask.

"Here, you'll need to put this on before going in the room- just for precaution."

"I will thanks."

"One more thing Sir, if she wakes up, do not let her talk much, she needs to rest."

Carl nodded and went in the room. As he opened the door, he noticed the lights were dimmed. The only sound in the room came from the heart monitor. She sleeping and looked so peaceful in spite of all she had gone through. He approached the bed and took her hand. He bent over and kissed her forehead, then sat in the chair next to the bed. He watched her chest rise with every breath she took. He closed his eyes and began to remember the moments they spent together. Exhaustion took over, and soon after he fell asleep still holding her hand.

***

CHAPTER 23

From the hall we could see Helen's small body covered in the blanket we brought her before surgery. Helen was peacefully sleeping. I knocked slightly at the glass, and when the nurse saw us she smiled and came over.

"You must be Helen's parents. She looks just like Dad."

"How is she doing?" I asked.

"She's doing amazingly well. She's a fighter, that's for sure. Her temperature is normal as well as her vital signs."

"Can we go in to see her?" Stephanie asked.

"I'm sorry, I wish I could let you, but the surgeon gave orders not to allow anyone in the room just yet. I'm confident that you'll be able to see her tomorrow. She's recovering very well."

"I understand. I miss her so much," Stephanie added.

"I'm sure but hang in there. It's better to wait a little longer and know that she's out of danger. The last thing we need is for her to develop an infection this early in the recovery. Her immune system is still weak. Now, if you have no more questions, I need to check on my other patients," she said, and went back to her station.

We stood outside the glass window for a few more minutes before heading back downstairs.

"What a week it's been. Can there be any more excitement?" Dad said joking.

"Who would ever know that Annabel turned out to be Fernando's mother," Laura said.

"Indeed, that was a shock to everyone," Stephanie replied.

"I'm not sure about you guys, but I can't wait to hear her story," Stephanie said.

I looked at her, but didn't say anything.

Stephanie and I spent the rest of the afternoon at my parent's house. Carl, still feeling awkward about his situation with Annabel, came by later in the evening for coffee.

"The doctor gave her something to relax and sleep. She was still sounding asleep when I left, but the nurse said she was recovering well and should be more alert tomorrow," Carl said.

"Carl, I know you're worried, but trust me, she's going to be all right," Laura said, trying to comforting him.

"I know. It's just that she's always been the strong one, always trying to lift my spirits, and now, she looks so vulnerable."

"I'm actually amazed how well she's done after what she's been through. Can you imagine? All this time she was baby-sitting her son's child, her granddaughter, unaware of it all, and then to find out she just saved her granddaughter's life," Antonio said.

***

Carl arrived at the hospital early the next morning where Stephanie was waiting for him in the lobby.

"Hey Dad, how did you sleep last night?"

"I barely slept. I tossed and turned all night. Thank goodness for high-tech coffee at the coffee shop. Where's Fernando?"

"That's the reason I was here waiting for you."

"Is everything all right?"

"Fernando went up to see Annabel. We called, and the nurse told us that she could have visitors."

"Hmm, why did he go there?" Carl asked frowning.

"He thought it was important that he spoke to her. He didn't sleep at all wondering what made her do what she did. Don't worry. He will be gentle with her."

"I see. Well it has to happen sooner or later."

Come on Dad; let's go have a cup of coffee and then go check on Helen. She was moved into a regular room this morning so now we can go in the room. I'm very excited."

"Well, sounds like everything is going back to normal for a change."

Stephanie smiled and holding his hand she led him into the elevator.

"You know something Dad?"

"What is that?

"I think Mom is smiling right now from up there."

"I want you to know that I'll never stop loving your mother."

"Dad, I know and trust me, I never had any doubt."

"It's just that I felt lonely, and Annabel has been good to me. It feels good to be loved again," he said then kissed her forehead.

Annabel woke up and looked around the room before she realized that Laura was sitting next to her bed. At first, she was confused and didn't know what was happening.

"Hey there, I thought you were going to wait until Christmas to wake up," Laura said smiling.

"Laura, how long have you been sitting here?"

"I got here an hour ago. I didn't want to wake you up."

"Laura, I…" Annabel started to explain, but Laura gestured with her finger not to talk.

"There's plenty of time to talk later. Right now, you need to rest. Your son and granddaughter are going to need you," Laura said with a smile.

"Tell me, how is Helen doing?"

"Oh, she's doing amazingly well for all she's gone through. The doctor thinks that she might be able to go home in a few days."

"I can't believe I found my son, Laura. I've been looking for him all these years. I never stopped thinking about him. I did what I had to do to save his life," she said, wiping the tears from her eyes.

"I know that. But right now, the most important thing is that you and Helen are on the mend. I spoke to the physician earlier. I hope you are not upset; I had to sign papers and lie. I told them I was your sister so they could give me information.

"Thank you, Laura. As for being my sister, well, you truly are. I'm so happy that my… Fernando found such a good family."

"You can say it, Annabel; you can say 'my son.' I haven't heard your side of the story, but based on what Carl told me, you did everything to save Fernando's life, and that my dear friend, makes you a good mother.

The door to the room opened slightly, and they heard a faint knock. Laura got up to see who was there. Fernando was standing outside looking a bit concerned. She looked at him and then back at Annabel.

"Is she awake?" he asked.

"Yes, she is, and she's looking forward to speaking to you."

"Mom, I'm scared."

"There's nothing to be afraid of. Annabel is a good woman, and she's your mother."

"But…"

"No 'but'. If you think I'm going to be jealous, you're wrong. I'll be proud to have an understanding son though."

"Mom..."

"All I want you to do is to listen to her side of the story, that's all"

"Thanks. You're the best mother anyone could ever have."

***

I went in the room and stared at her. Annabel pulled herself up in bed and sat up against the pillows. At first, I didn't know what to say. I felt compassion for this woman who just hours before, learned that she was my mother.

"Hi, how are you feeling?" I asked to break the silence.

"Much better than the doctors anticipated. Yesterday, they didn't think I was going to make it," she said with a faint smile.

I approached the bed and surprised her by bending over and kissing her forehead.

"Helen is doing amazingly well too, thanks to your generosity. Her recovery has surprised the doctors," I said.

"She is such a strong little girl. I'm so happy that I was able to save her life, not just for me, but for her family as well.

"I think she's as strong as her grandmother, don't you think?"

"Well, Laura is strong and a good woman," Annabel said.

"Actually, I was talking about you, Annabel. She is after all your granddaughter."

My comment brought tears to her eyes, and she was at a loss for words. She knew that was my way of telling her that I was not angry with her.

Thirty years ago when you were born, I had to make the worse decision any woman could make: to give away her child."

"Annabel, I want you to know I hold nothing against you. On the contrary, I'm so thankful for the family I ended up with and for that I'll always be grateful."

"I was nineteen years old," Annabel said. "My parents had died, and the only person left was your father. He was a good man, but he started drinking and doing drugs with his friends. When he found out I was pregnant, he became angry and abusive. Against his will,

I decided to carry you for nine months, without his help. I though that once you were born he would change. I was wrong. By the time you were born, he was so deep into drugs that he didn't even notice you, except when you cried at night, and then he became angry and even threatened to harm you. That's when I made the decision to give you away. I wouldn't have forgiven myself if something happened to you. The rest you already know."

I sat quietly listening to her story. At times, my eyes filled with tears. I could see how hard it was for her having to tell me that my father wanted nothing to do with me.

"I went from living with my parents to being with your father, and so I never really learned to survive on my own, let alone with a newborn. I thought hard and long, and when

I made my decision, I made it based on your safety and your future. Not once, did I think about myself."

I stood up and walked toward the window without saying a word. I looked outside toward the lake... needing time to take it all in. Not wanting Annabel to think I was upset with her, I soon turned back to face her.

"Annabel," I said, pausing for a brief moment. "I could never hate you for what you did. You gave me a chance for a better life. My parents are the best parents anyone could ever dream of and for that I will always be grateful. I always wondered who my real parents were. I thought about you constantly, and of course, I wondered why you did what you did. But now that I know, I completely understand."

"Fernando, I'm so sorry. Please forgive me. I didn't know what else to do at that time"

"Stop, Annabel, there's nothing to forgive. In any case, there's a lot to thank you for. As I told you, you gave me a chance at a better life and now, you gave me back my daughter, and your granddaughter has a second chance at life. How can we ever repay you for what you have done? These two events are proof enough that you never did stop loving me."

I approached the bed. She started crying; I felt the need to hold her tight in my arms.

"My baby, thank you God for bringing him back to me."

"I love you Mom," I replied giving her a gentle hug and a kiss, tears sliding down my cheeks as I cried with her.

***

CHAPTER 24

"Hurry up, Annabel. You're going to be late," Laura called out.

"I'm coming, I'm coming. This gown must have shrunk since I last tried it on. Here, help me with the zipper."

"Are you sure it's the gown? I do recall you tasting about ten different cake pieces before you settled on the chocolate mocha cake for the wedding."

"I did not," Annabel complained.

"All right, here you go. Now, let's hurry. We don't want to make the groom wait too long.

He's already called three times to make sure you didn't change your mind at the last minute."

"He did what? Are you serious? Oh Lord, that man is unbelievable."

Stephanie walked in the room and her eyes filled with tears.

"Honey, what's wrong?" Annabel asked.

"You look so beautiful, Annabel," Stephanie replied.

"Thank you. I still think I'm a bit too old to be wearing a traditional wedding gown."

"Oh now Annabel, stop it. Stephanie is right. You do look wonderful. I think our son Fernando is going to be proud to walk you down the aisle."

"Never in my wildest dreams had I thought this day would come, Laura. The funny thing is that my stepdaughter is also my daughter-in-law which makes Helen twice my granddaughter!"

Fernando could hear laughter inside the room. He knocked at the door and let himself in. The women were laughing hysterically.

Ladies, you are having too much fun, and we are a getting late. The limo is already…"

Fernando was at a lost for words when he turned and saw Annabel standing by the mirror.

"Mom," he said, with a proud smile on his face, "you look beautiful."

"Stop it, you're making me cry, and I just put on mascara," she replied, with tears in her eyes.

He approached her and gave her a kiss. Laura pulled the flower arrangement from the box on the dresser. After a few minor details, they headed for the church.

The church was decorated in lavender and pink roses. Carl had been standing by the altar for the past ten minutes with Antonio by his side. He kept looking at his watch wondering what was taking them so long.

"Relax Carl. Women are always late on their wedding day. I swear they do it purposely to see us sweat," Antonio said.

"Yeah well, she's five minutes late. Do you think she backed out? I mean, she is a beautiful young woman, and I'm up in age you know. Or what if something happened to her? I mean, she almost died two months ago. Do you think we should call and check on them?" Carl said, checking his watch again.

Just as he was about to speak again, the church organ started to play, everyone in the church stood up and looked toward the back as the two doors opened up.

As the music started to play, Helen, her cheeks rosy with health, started walking down the isle. She was wearing a long lavender dress with a pink ribbon around her waist. Her basket was filled with pink roses and lavender. She couldn't stop smiling while looking at the guests, and they were smiling back at her. Stephanie, the matron of honor, walked down the aisle followed by Laura and two other bridesmaids. At Carl's request, Antonio, the best man, was to be his only attendant. He had been Carl's source of strength and comfort during all the painful moments, and he didn't want anyone else by his side now that he was about to get another chance at happiness.

Carl took a big deep breath and his eyes opened wide when he saw Annabel.

"My brother, here comes your bride," Antonio said giving Carl a quick hug.

"Boy, she is one heck of a bride," he said with pride.

'Carl, behave. Remember where you standing," Antonio replied.

Carl looked at him and both started giggling.

***

Gracious and smiling, Annabel walked down the aisle by my side. I could see how nervous she was; she reached for my hand for a moment and clutched it tightly before taking my arm. When we approached the altar, I turned to her and gave her a kiss.

"Carl, I give you my mother's hand. I trust you will make her happy," I told him shaking his hand.

"I will son, I promise," he replied.

Carl took Annabel's hand and led her up to the altar where Father Sullivan was waiting to marry the couple.

At the end of the ceremony, Father Sullivan blessed the newly married couple and presented them to us, their family and friends. Everyone joined in the congratulatory round of applause; Carl and Annabel were in love and it showed.

"Fernando, your mother looks so happy. I'm glad they found each other. My father really needed her," Stephanie said, as we watched watching the newly married couple's first dance.

"Are you all right with this? I mean, I know how much you love your mother," I asked her.

"I will never stop loving my mother, but life has to go on, and seeing my father happy is on my list of top priorities right now. Besides, Annabel is an extraordinary woman, and I couldn't think of anyone else who could take that position."

"I agree. It's so strange though. My mother just married my father-in-law."

"What's so strange about it?"

Well, think about it. That makes you my stepsister," I said laughing.

"Fernando, Oh Lord, stop that!

"I was joking, relax and enjoy the moment."

"You kids look like you're enjoying yourselves," Antonio said as he approached our table with Laura.

"Fernando is being funny, that's all," Stephanie replied.

I'm so happy for both of them. I think they are going to be extremely happy. I do have to confess; I'm extremely jealous of their honeymoon trip to Italy," Laura commented.

Now that you mention it, Mom, I forgot to tell you that if you don't hurry and pack, you are going to miss your flight tomorrow," I replied, reaching inside my jacket.

"What are you talking about?" she asked, her face showing her confusion. Carl and Annabel approached the table just as I placed a couple of airline tickets in front of Antonio.

"My dear sister Laura," Annabel said, "Carl and I have gone through a lot this past year.

You two have been our support and our shoulder to cry on. We didn't know how else to thank you."

"But…"

"Let me finish," she said. "You gave up so much of your own lives and your time from each other to help keep this family together. Now that our lives are back on track, it's time for us to repay your kindness."

"But, I don't understand. You gave us the best gift of all. You gave our Helen another chance at life. You owe us nothing. And this is your honeymoon. We can't possibly go with you," my father said. "Oh the heck with that! Who said you couldn't. Annabel and I talked about it, and we think it would be wonderful if you came with us. Besides, weren't you the one who told me that on your wedding day you had only enough money to go down the Cape for your honeymoon?" Carl asked.

"Well yes, but…"

"Well, it's time you enjoy a second honeymoon in Italy.

"But this must have cost you a fortune," Laura said.

"Laura dear," my father-in-law said, "Rachel and I saved money for retirement, and she wasn't able to enjoy it. There's a lesson to be learned here. Enjoy today while you can because you don't know what tomorrow is going to bring."

"My heart is pounding right now. I don't know what to say. I've never been out of the country."

"Grandma, are you going to travel by plane?" Helen asked. She was so excited by the thought.

"Yes my sweet girl, I guess I am," Laura replied.

"Stephanie, I saved this piece of music for us. Would you and Helen care to dance with me?" I asked.

"I was wondering when you were going to ask," she replied.

When everyone saw us dancing, they all joined us on the dance floor. Helen was having the time of her life going from one hand to another laughing and singing...

"It's good to be home again... it really is!"

End

ABOUT THE AUTHOR

Alberto Mercado was born in Puerto Rico and moved to the States in 1985.

He resides in Sturbridge, Mass. He balances his life between working fifty hours a week, family, friends and photography: one of his favorite hobbies.

His first book titled "From Ashes To Dreams; My Life, My Story." was a work in the making for a long time becoming a reality in the spring of 2009 when he decided to publish it. The book earned him great reviews from readers and local newspapers.

"I love stories with a happy ending, that's just the way I am. I'm having the time of my life writing stories, and I will continue as long as people continue to enjoy reading my books."

OTHER TITLES BY THE AUTHOR

"From Ashes to Dreams; My Life, My Story."
(English Version)

"De Cenizas A Suenos; My Vida, My Historia"
(Spanish Version)

**Available in paperback, Amazon.com "Kindle" and Barnes & Nobles "Pubit."*

64

de in the USA
Charleston, SC
27 October 2010